DEATH ON THE
DRIVING RANGE

Off-duty PC Arthur Root is playing a round at Wolvers, his local golf club. However, he soon finds himself back on duty when a JCB driver working there digs up the body of a man. Root protects the excavated area as a crime scene. The man had been murdered, and is identified as Roger Hancock, a former member of the club. When there is a second brutal murder, involving many members of the golf club — Root himself becomes implicated . . .

BRIAN BALL

DEATH ON THE DRIVING RANGE

Complete and Unabridged

LINFORD
Leicester

First published in Great Britain

First Linford Edition
published 2009

British Library CIP Data

Ball, Brian, *1932 –*
    Death on the driving range.—Large print ed.—
Linford mystery library
    1. Murder—Investigation—Fiction
    2. Detective and mystery stories
    3. Large type books
    I. Title
    823.9'12 [F]

ISBN 978–1–84782–522–3

Published by
F. A. Thorpe (Publishing)
Anstey, Leicestershire

Set by Words & Graphics Ltd.
Anstey, Leicestershire
Printed and bound in Great Britain by
T. J. International Ltd., Padstow, Cornwall

This book is printed on acid-free paper

1

The jagged outline of the castellations and crenellations of the eighteenth-century iron-master's former mansion that was now the clubhouse, if not the glory, of Wolvers Hall, could just be discerned. It lay in the distance, through the towering stand of ancient elms that fringed the putting green, from where Arthur Root stood on the seventeenth tee. He marvelled at his good fortune. Tee, and tea, that was the way his thoughts ran.

And yet. Was it all too good to last?

Maybe, thought Root, much later, he was too much exposed at that time to the aura of someone who was near him and who had been in the thick of blood and violence and despair, someone he cared for.

There were others who experienced premonitions of what would come to bloody the scene, shatter the prospect and mock the idyll; yet who paid them heed on a day of such Autumnal promise? Some of the members did. And the staff who served them.

Angie Knight, for one, had put aside any deeper if not finer feelings she might have felt. She had long since decided that golf was no longer for her.

A full-bodied woman of thirty-eight, childless by choice, still pretty and with fine tapering ankles, she knew that she was a gift to men. Willingly given, too. Just now the tall, square-bodied chisel-faced recently appointed professional was to benefit from her revived and urgent needs. 'Mick?'

His car was in the lot, the big Lagonda, bright blue, canvas hood down, the bonnet cool to her touch. She could smell the leather and the lingering aroma of his last cigar mingling with a hint of Aramis.

'Mick!'

Angie tried to calm herself. Was this latest involvement to last?

★ ★ ★

Out beyond the bounds of the club, an old man and a dog were looking hard at a grove of long-since coppiced willows around a stone-built farm with the roof fallen in. Small, brown forms swarmed over the ruin.

Fred, peering through the John Deere's screen, old and angry with himself, gave the horn a mournful blast, then berated the huge, skinny bag of bones that had won him quite a few quid over the years out at the dog track Thrybergh way. 'You could have gone an' nipped 'em. I didn't see 'em come. Brown little buggers. Must be foreign-like. Did you catch gold on skinny lad's neck, 'Itler? Who'd be a sodding greenkeeper? Never a minute's peace.'

★   ★   ★

Peace and contentment were fine, Root decided, but there was a slow foursome in front: patience was a necessity right now. Most coppering was not dissimilar in that. So, wait. The wait lengthened, and the quiet calm of the early

3

September day was gone.

'Big blade,' said his young playing companion.

'Has to be. Lot of earth to shift.'

The levelling of Anglers Kop was not halfway accomplished.

Back to tea. Tea would be good, he thought. Tea and crumpets, brought by the steward's stunning new blonde-haired find and everyone's favourite waitress, Josie, a local girl who had a laugh like a drain, as they said in that part of the world, and also an eye for brisk young fellows like wide-shouldered Gary Brand, who stood beside the tee now waiting for him to drive down the bright sunlit fairway with his powerful, steady swing and coolly judged placement.

* * *

By chance, Josie Marsden's keen young eyes had picked out a gap in the chestnuts that would have been a photographer's ideal frame for the seventeenth; it had given her a perfect view of Gary's tall figure. She found a quiet corner: keyed

4

the number and told her mate at the cake-shop in Gritmarsh just how she felt on seeing that tall, crew-cut and bronzed newly returned soldier. 'I had to rush in, I'd've had the old biddies gawping, past it, them, and well you know how it takes you — I fancied him something rotten, Eileen. What? Yes, course! Ooh, slag!'

The two old women that Josie considered past it looked out over the course, but could see little of the back six holes. Not for them a glimpse of the tensions developing on the two penultimate holes. Both knew, however, that Alice's partner was due back at the clubhouse soon.

'Your Ted looks well,' advanced Alice's large, sparkling-eyed arthritic friend Ivy. 'Considering. How's his angina?'

'He's champion,' asserted Alice, hoping it was so. There were depths to her partner she could not quite see into. 'And his heart's in good standing, as it should be. On my bill, please.'

Josie, still joyous from using up the last of the credit on her mobile, had come to clear up. Her skin glowed in the sunlight. She smiled with delight as she went.

'Saw her eyeing up that young lad with Arthur Root', said Ivy, turning swiftly to the next item. 'Who would he be then, Alice? Seems a decent sort. Well set. Looks lively, too. Yes?'

Josie had already determined that she would find out.

★ ★ ★

Gary had not seen her. Golf was all: for now.

'Two hundred and ten yards, as usual,' he said. 'Wish I could place them like you, just steady, all grooved like down a rifle barrel, nothing flash or smash, fairish height and no hook or drift. Steady old Arthur. Good 'un, always was, always will be, there when you need him, that's what mum says. Just you watch our Arthur and you'll soon forget that nasty business over there.'

He talked too much, of course, but it was understandable.

Nervy. That would be his recent service in Basra.

'Great swing, Arthur, I mean it. It's not

a long backswing, just like Mick Summers says when he's trying to stop me jerking the wood round my neck like a tennis racquet. Slow and steady. Never seen you hook, not once.'

To add to Root's irritation, the JCB driver chose that moment to rev his engine, sending the decibel-rate soaring. He glanced over to the gaudy yellow earth-mover. The blade gouged forward massively. Soil flowed. And still his wife's favourite friend's lad rattled on.

'Never a fade you didn't want either. As for a hook — '

'Gary, learn this,' growled Arthur Root. 'Don't use that word again! You do not tell a man on the tee that he won't hook. Ever! I don't want my swing analysing by anyone, especially a lad I'm putting up for full membership. And that won't happen till the flag goes up again, Gary. So concentrate on ingratiating yourself with everyone, me most of all, got it? Right?'

'I was only — '

'Right, lad?'

Gary maintained a discreet silence.

Root watched as he placed the yellow plastic peg carefully, seat the oldish Titleist in the cup — then, jobless, membership-aspirant and shell-shocked Gary hit, a belter way past Arthur Root's usual length off the tee. He was a natural with a club, as he had proved to be with weaponry.

'You don't want that one back, Gary,' Root managed to get out encouragingly, if still a bit close-mouthed.

'Lucky,' said Gary. 'Only one I've hit on the sweet spot this round.'

They progressed down the fairway in company, but each deep in thought. Root realised he was drifting. Work filtered through. There was the cannabis he suspected to be ready for the local market somewhere in his area. *Skunk*. That was it, nasty word. Could the local kids be using? Were pushers sidling up to the teenagers streaming out of the local comp? *On my patch?* But that wasn't Root's only worry. It seemed likely as Root had painfully learned from far too many close encounters with domestic tribulation, that with Gary fresh home, he and his mum had a problem.

But Arthur Root wouldn't spoil the lad's day.

He seemed more relaxed now. Was he?

* * *

It could be, Gary told himself, a damn sight worse. But I'm alive, a lance-jack no longer, but right here in South Yorkshire, admittedly with an uncertain future to consider: yet with Josie's firm, swaying and delightfully sinuous way of filling her black waitress's dress to contemplate: and all amongst green, rolling fairways under a blue sky — all of it not in a grim cold desert, but in England, he thought, just as the whooping began.

The row from the big earth-moving vehicle — the source of the loud, bleating intermittent whoops — was all-pervading.

'Devil of a row,' growled Root, voicing loudly his sympathy with his more senior fellow-members in the gesticulating foursome ahead. 'What's got into that JCB driver? Gone on strike? Wasp stung him?'

'I think it's more than that, Arthur. I'd say it's trouble.'

'What d'you mean, trouble, Gary?'

'Three whoops, Arthur. It's the international distress signal. All else fails, coms gone, that's it. Heard it too often lately.'

2

'Of course, Gary. I hadn't forgotten, just wasn't expecting anything. Three whoops, repeated. Some sort of trouble, yes, has to be. We'll go and meet him. Hey, there! We're coming over.'

Arthur, thought Gary, wasn't as quick or as sharp as he remembered him from when he himself was just a kid. Arthur Root then, tall and wide, not a spare ounce on him, was his hero. Quiet and calm, strong as any light-heavy Gary had ever seen fight, he was as sharp as a starved ferret then when it came to facts and events. Was he getting a bit shaky with age?

'Arthur, what is ailing him, do you think' he asked, as the JCB's driver reeled away from the big all-purpose vehicle. He was obviously perturbed by the driver's plight.

'He'll tell us soon enough. Come on. He's had it.'

The shortish older man stopped and almost fell to the ground. Root steadied him. 'All right, lad, let it all out, all of it. You're going to be better when it's gone. Finished now?'

The old man vomited again.

'He's in shock, Arthur. Sit down, will you, please. What's your name, old son? I know, something bad, isn't it? So you're on with a job, and just take your time and here's the local Community bobby, you'll have heard of him if you don't actually know him, right? Here's P.C. Root, yes, he's a policeman, he's here to help, just tell us your name first and we'll start from there. You all right with this old anorak round your shoulders?'

Gary was doing well. But then he'd been a medic with the Terriers.

The old man was now focusing. First on Gary, then on Root himself.

'Name, is it now? I'm Owen. Owen Burroughs. Driver for Mr. Knight. Come to level that bit of a hill for you, haven't I?'

He was looking intently at the massive girdering of the JCB, still grunting with

12

power, but blade up now. Owen shook as he pointed. 'Near took the head clean off, but I spotted it, just. Stopped, got the blade up.'

Head? Had he heard aright?

'Take your time, Owen. Just tell me.'

'He'll blame me, he will,' muttered Owen Burroughs. 'Bobby-trouble he could do without. Wish he'd given that daft new lad from Hagthorpe the job. Never seen anything like it outside the horror stuff on telly after midnight. Not watching any more, am I?'

Gary heard the last bit, but he was unheeding of chance remarks.

'Your job, Arthur, not mine,' he said.

A head, thought Root. Knight would certainly not like it, for it most definitely was, as Burroughs put it, bobby-trouble. Could it be a part of the complex mythology and legend of Anglers Kop — ? Maybe a long-dead barbarian still with his golden armlets and iron-bossed shield? Or a Roman legionary? He moved fast and identified the relict for what it was.

'Dear god,' he said aloud.

There was a human skull faced away from him, but not a decayed, ancient carapace, no. Not Roman or Iron Age Briton. A human being's head poked like some outlandish fungus from the disturbed Kop's grey-black, arid soil. And not all that long dead, either. There was still hair about the crown. Bizarrely, there was also an arm sticking out of the soil. Root wanted a pen in his grasp and the notebook from his tunic pocket. There. Windcheater.

Automatically, he scribbled down the main facts. Time, date, place. Present were the following. I identified provisionally what I took to be. There was more. Down it went, very briefly, but a true and indisputable log. It would soon be needed. Still more.

'Now,' he muttered. 'What's that?'

And what was that showing an inch or two above the untidy heap of gritty soil? Metal, shiny metal. Old? An ancient artefact? No, not anywhere nearly right. Any notion of an archaeological find could be dismissed.

So could any thought of doing more

14

than his immediate duty, which was to establish an authoritative presence; and diligently keep prying eyes and contaminating feet and fingers away.

As First Officer Attending, he could not leave here. It was his primary duty to guard the *corpus delecti*, the most important piece of evidence there would ever be in this case. So here I stay.

'Gary, get over to Mr. Wynne-Fitzpatrick there. Setting off down the eighteenth. Call him 'Major, sir', he'll respond quicker. You've seen him before, and you should be seeing him at five today, but I suspect that's off now. Tell him — ask him — to hold up play at the sixteenth. He'll send the greenkeeper out on his tractor, most likely. Can't ask him here, it's too up and down, his angina won't stand the strain. Nor his gout, which must be giving him gip right now they're finishing. You've got young legs. Say I want play stopped before the seventeenth tee.' Gary looked as though he had suggestions. Root looked around the macabre scene. 'Just wait a moment.'

This was old bones; not millenially-old

bones such as would bedazzle old Josh Jowett: but conceivably a crime scene. He'd be exceeding his authority by quarantining the members. Yet there was a middle way. 'No,' he said abruptly. 'Names of everyone here. All the staff remain, no exceptions. On my authority.' He already had his police radiophone ready to report what was looking increasingly like a serious incident. 'Away with you, now, Gary, quick about it. You did well, lad, with old Owen here. Go!'

The last remarks were lost, since Gary had a good turn of speed. Root returned briefly to check on the JCB driver, a better colour beginning to return to his pasty, green-jowled face. No heart attack, no serious distress, he told himself. 'Just stay there, Owen,' he ordered. 'You'll be right.'

He strode quickly back and reached inside the cab of the earth-moving dinosaur and turned off the power. Then he stood back, again careful to avoid contaminating the area. 'Been there some time,' he found himself muttering aloud. 'Just bones and cartilage and rags of skin.

And what is that?'

He looked more closely at the find. A rusted knob of once-highly-finished black-lacquered metal poked through the disturbed soil, much like the handle of an early Hoover. 'Odd,' he said aloud. 'Bones and metal, and all buried under Anglers Kop for God knows how long. Or why.'

'You got it worked out, Arthur? What it is?'

Gary was back sooner than Root had anticipated. He was looking down at the find. 'It's part of an old metal-detector. Electropulse. Sends a signal in a cone down about eight inches. Be about a couple of hundred quid twenty years ago. Before ground-penetrating radar units, but pretty good. Could be an Arado. They cost real money.'

Old technology? Root had seen their like in use before. 'You'd know. Didn't your dad buy you one when you were a kid?'

'Buy! Doubtful, that, Arthur. I got it for a ninth birthday present. He'd gone for mum again, and this was his way of getting back into the house. And at mum's benefits and allowances. And her money from that skivvying job, and anything else he could lay his hands on. He'd have nicked the detector from somewhere. Maybe robbed some kid out in the fields looking for Roman coins, like the rest of us. Only thing he ever gave me that I wanted to use. Gave me a taster of what was to come, I suppose.'

'Yes. Basra. You'd do a course on mines, then, that kind of ordnance? In UK?' said Root, thinking that Gary had seen a hell of a lot for a twenty-three year old South Yorkshire lad.

'There wasn't time. We got rushed out quick. More or less learned on the job. By then it wasn't mines. No time for detection — they had all the remote control technology they needed from over the border.'

Root shook his head. Someone had been looking for ancient treasure here. What else would they bring a mine detector for? And where would that lead him, Constable Root?

'It's going to be a messy business,' he

said. 'It gets a lot of publicity, this sort of thing. Everyone wants in on it. Easy money, they think. Make your fortune with a turn of the spade.'

'Or a buzz from the magic wand. Some people get lucky.'

'He didn't. Poor sod.'

'So what next?' said Gary.

'Hang about. You'll be used to that, I expect. Do nowt till you're told, then just say what you've seen, short and clear and maybe we'll get to the clubhouse before all the crumpets have gone.'

'So what's happened here, do you think, Arthur?'

'Not for me to say, lad. Nor you. But we'll find out. We always do.'

A loud voice hailed them. The voice of command. 'Anything else, Arthur?' A man of two distinct persuasions, thought Root: lowering and jovial, mercurial and morbid. That was the nature of Major Alfred Wynne-Fitzpatrick, MC and well earned so it was said. This was a man who had commanded a biggish force back in the Falklands campaign; not that he ever spoke of it.

19

'I don't want any sightseers, Major!'

'Any *what*!'

This was not a parade ground, Root told himself. He prodded Gary's well-muscled shoulder. 'Get yourself across again and explain that I respectfully ask the major as Captain of the club to make sure that no one comes out here. Say I said it's official business. And tell him he's in charge. Now, off.'

And soon I won't be, thought Root, for here came the forerunners.

A natty new Ford Focus, bright blue, swished along the newly-asphalted drive, not fast, investigative officers come to establish a presence with no fuss at all: two, no three, for the one in the back was small. Old Owen Burroughs watched the car till it was hidden by the sycamores at the end of the drive.

'This the poliss, is it?'

'Expect so,' said Root. 'We'll just wait and see. All right?'

'I just want out. Skulls aren't in my job specification, right? I just use heavy tools. Who, for Michael and Mary's sake did I dig up?'

This was for the experts, thought Root, empathizing.

'Not our worry, Owen.'

Soon, there'd be a CID contingent, an ambulance and the Home Office pathologist and as much and as many of the Support Services as headquarters deemed necessary. Root wondered how the various officials and employees would be coping up at the clubhouse.

Secretary Phil Church would have to handle it. And how would he cope?

Not well at all at first. Right. And who would begin the investigation?

Root thought he knew one shape in the recently arrived police car, a dedicated real-ale fancier called Strapp. He rather hoped that it was Sergeant Strapp he had glimpsed, Izzy Strapp from Welwyn Garden City. South Yorkshire fitted him like an old worn glove, the beer, the barbed and lateral bleak humour of the locals, and the cheap housing.

'A puzzle for you Izzy,' he said aloud. 'And me.'

Arthur Root looked again at the marrow-like skull, with its shreds of leathery skin still clinging to the lower jaw. Who were you? he asked. And why here, at Wolvers?

So, at the clubhouse: what?

★ ★ ★

'Oh, bugger,' the pro was saying, hearing his assistant yelling his name. Young Tony Beevers knew quite well where he was and what he was doing. 'Sounds important, my love.'

'Bugger too,' said Mrs. Angela Knight, gathering garments. 'Anyway, it's coming on to rain and my hair's going to be a right mess, you and your big hands, Mick. Can't say I like the sound of this.' She knew about sudden emergencies, and had had quite enough of them. 'This is serious, is it? I mean, the lad knows better than to come here, doesn't he? What, you off?'

'Back in a second or two.'

'Left alone again,' she said. 'Poor little Angie.'

Trouble?

Mick Summers hugged her briefly, then

tore out of the thicket that concealed the interior of the folly from a casual inspection, and called back to his assistant,

'Panic over, Tony, I'm here.'

'It isn't. You're wanted in the bar, right away. Phil's there. And some others, all in a stew. Want to know why?'

★　★　★

'Couldn't be worse,' Phil Church was saying, as he waited for those he had summoned or whose presence he had deferentially requested. Better to have them together and give them what news there was, and then keep them together as long as they were willing to stay to see what would break next.

'Bliss!' he called to the steward. 'When's Mick Summers coming? You have told him to get here right away, haven't you?'

'Done that, Mr. Church. Anything to drink just now?'

'Drink? No, I don't want anything to drink, do I! Ah, Alice!'

She had no intention of leaving summarily or quickly.

'Let's be positive, Phil. It may not be murder, but we all like a good mystery, don't we? And on our doorstep, so to speak.'

'I suppose Arthur Root's done all the right things, had to be done officially, but God knows I hope they can get all this cleared up soon. We don't want the place cluttered up with large bobbies' feet for long, do we?'

'Brought you your gin, Mr. Church,' Charlie Bliss offered, who hadn't been told to. 'Large one. And again for you, Ma'am? Yes? Very well.'

'Yes, get it cleared up,' said Phil Church, cradling the glass. 'Today.'

'That's not the way it's going to happen.'

3

'No Phil,' this woman was telling him, with an air of knowledgeable authority. 'You can't wish them away once those big official feet get through the door. You hoped they would pop a few questions and then go away. That's not how a police investigation works, take my word. They come back again and again.'

'Well, you know how these things work, being on the Bench. I suppose. So what's to be done? How do we handle the police?'

'Wait. And we don't. But I rather think the Major will know. Better have a large brandy ready, Phil,' said Alice. 'Doesn't do his gout any good, but it'll improve his temper. Bliss, this is on me.'

'Yes, Ma'am.' grovelled Bliss, who was very careful to be scrupulously polite to all the lady members. One ill-judged word, and he d behind the bar in some lousy pub down the town. 'Balloon glass, of course, Ma'am.'

* ★ ★

'I'm not hanging around, not me. Not with the police involved. What about Tony? Can he keep his mouth shut, Mick?'

She was in the car park, keys to the silver Aston Martin in her hand.

Summers grimaced. It was serious, and it meant trouble. 'He's a bright kid. Knows when not to say too much. But I've got to get moving. I told you, this is more than serious, it's a bloody calamity, Angie. It's a corpse. A dead man.'

Not entirely coincidentally, Angie Knight's thoughts were on just that subject. Mick's lugubrious expression cheered her. She had been mulling over with some pleasure how absolutely convenient for her the news of an early death could be: that of her now-separated spouse. Quick and not too long delayed. With pain, if possible. Not murder, no. Yet a natural death was too good for him, she opined frequently to her intimates. She hoped a different kind of ending would take care of her ex-husband. Lingering and painful. Say a bad car wreck. She worked positively towards his downfall, so far without success. Why should the manipulative sod get into a decent club — it was like letting in a rat with rabies. Meanwhile, she could do without any complications in her life. 'How's Wednesday looking. Mick?'

'Well, why not, my love?'

'If you don't get the push before then.' Then she added hastily, 'Just joking. I don't want you out. You're too much of a good thing, Mick. I'll make sure you're all right, if anyone starts noseying around you-know-what.'

'Ah. Yes. Quite, Angie.'

Summers did know-what. His debts. They were accumulating, what with the interest Betsafe charged.

'I'm a fixture here, Angie. Yours. Want to put me on your mantelpiece?'

She demonstrated her feelings in unsubtle ways there and then.

'Randy brute, aren't you?' smiled Mrs. Knight. 'Real pro at it too.'

'All I want, a deader on the practice-ground. There goes my lessons for the week. Just what I need.'

*　*　*

Phil Church recalled what he knew of previous encounters with a sudden death at Wolvers. He would take Alice Godalming's advice. That was how he had become a successful and fairly rich businessman: an instinct for sound reasoning, together with his native caution, had done the trick. It would now, he was sure. Spread the load. And go easy on the gin.

'You're right about this, Alice,' he said. 'We need the Major's advice.'

The timing was impeccable.

' — ah, Major! Here, Alice's idea. Said you'll need it.'

'Major! So glad you're here,' said Mrs. Godalming. 'Now, tell us all what's happened. But Ted, where's he got to?'

'Bless you, Alice, so kind of you, always said Ted was a lucky devil! I needed that, so I did! Well, he's told you there's a casualty — a set of bones — out at the diggings on the Kop? Said he would. Get on that little blower of his. I don't get on with these tiny plastic things. An all-fired damnable nuisance, couldn't finish the round, doing well with the short irons, d'you see, wasn't I, we were one up one to go, all we needed was a half, but that gets no fiver apiece for myself and Ted, does it, an unfinished round, eh? He's showering, slow. Should have been in the mob, that'd have shifted him — ! Where was I? Ah, phone! Things need sorting out instanter, got to talk to the right people. Get to the top, you see, before the balloon goes up, as we used to say — Phil. I'll need your office.'

Church knew exactly why.

'But at least tell us what you've seen, will you?' pleaded Alice. 'Oh, the hell with it, I will have another. Major; don't rush off just yet, please. Phil and I quite appreciate that you were about to contain matters, but at least wait for a moment to tell us what these ghastly matters are. Major? I am right, Phil?'

'Of course, Alice. Alf?'

'Of course, damned impolite of me! My apologies, my dear! All right, it's a wretched business. The body's been in the ground for years, no telling how long, according to what Root's lad's just told me — Gary's his name, been in the military, as you two know, so he's up to the mark, knows how to make a report — yes, he's seen the remains. It's all that's left of some poor devil. Old bones, according to Arthur Root. A big skull, prominent eyebrows and jaw, so it will be a man's.'

'Did you see the bones yourself, Major?' said Alice Godalming.

'No. Not my place to. Arthur Root doesn't want anyone trampling around before the specialists come. Quite right too. Anyway, I wasn't going back up that hill and down again onto the old Cartwright land. Told my team we're best out of it. Better here. Yes, Bliss. All of us.'

Phil Church decided that, on balance, this was best left to the Wolvers Captain. Alice thought about criminals she had sent down. Charlie Bliss felt a wonderful glow of importance. He would get to know all he could, and he would tell so little. Until he saw an advantage in so doing. He served the drinks, then he pointed to the large bay window. 'Police car just arrived, Ma'am. Gentlemen.'

Major Wynne-Fitzpatrick grabbed the recharged balloon glass and departed with a growl of pain and a heavy clumping of his good foot. 'Be right back, Phil. Alice!'

Bliss knew what was in the offing. In a minute or two, he would be out of the action. He probably wouldn't get as much as a glimpse at the find. Nevertheless, it was turning out to be an excellent day, except, of course, for the luscious Josie's contemptuous brush-off; but this looked to be the real thing. The Secretary looked to be off-balance, which was how any minor crisis affected him, so he chanced his luck.

'So we've turned up a bit of history, have we, Mr. Church? What is it, a leftover from the fight on the Kop? Yonks back? The Romans and the Ancient Brits, would you say? Mr. Chips would know, Mrs. Godalming. He's the member to ask, right, sir?'

'Bliss is right, Alice. And that would be Mr. Jowett to you. Damn it, he was here an hour or two back, said he'd play the front six by himself, his usual when he doesn't want company — where is the old fossil, Bliss?'

'Can't say, sir. Only yourselves around, just now.'

'Phil, be discreet!'

He couldn't. 'I'll find him! He's the expert. Heard him talking archaeology for hours. Alice, my dear, Josh could have us out of this mess in a minute!'

'Phil, we'll catch up with him another time. The police certainly will.'

'No, this is Club business. Now's the time! Got to be done. The Major's right — get things sorted out.' And he was away, in Alice Godalming's estimation away and rudely, into the great entrance hall, presumably making for the locker-room. 'Where's Josh Jowett?' she heard him calling as he went. 'Anybody know?'

★　★　★

Three of the slow foursome were finishing dressing. Ted Jones almost ready. 'Ted? JJ? What do you think? He's gone, has he?'

Ted Jones, sleeking down his thick black hair with Brilliantine, thought he might have seen his car making a smooth but swift exit.

'Didn't see him in here, Phil. Hared off, has he? Wish I could. Alice into the gin?'

★　★　★

'Who's this?' said Gary, trying. Root glanced at his watch. Things didn't happen immediately in any investigation; but they happened. He was surprised to see that almost half-an-hour had passed since that three-note repeated bellowing had flooded the back six with its mournful intelligence. 'The brass?'

It would not be a member of the more senior ranks of the Criminal Investigation Department. Not for old bones haphazardly discovered.

'Not the top brass, no. Middling. You'll be late for tea.'

Tea was dinner for most in South Yorkshire. A full meal, served usually at six-thirty. Ah, well. Tea would keep. 'Gary, you keep out of it. Speak when you're spoken to, otherwise say nowt.'

And here came the first, a comfortably built sergeant Root knew well. He waved to Root, who indicated the find. It was the driver he'd glimpsed in the Focus who was unfamiliar to him. Young, slim, and female. She looked a bit like his Beth, he thought.

'Let,' he said, very quietly, 'the wild rumpus begin.'

* * *

'Inspector to see you, Mr. Church,' called Bliss. He couldn't help adding, 'In a hurry too. Can't see why. Only old Roman bones, isn't it?'

Alice Godalming patted the Secretary's hand. 'Here's the Law.'

A very tall youngish detective inspector strode into the large, sunlit lounge. He had a confident air about him, which Josie, peeping round the back of the bar, quite approved of. Bit old, though. And he'd be wed. Not an insurmountable problem. Well-spoken, and that made him intriguing. Yorkshire, but smooth, no edges.

He smiled at Alice as the introductions were concluded.

Alice said nothing. The DIs now looked far too damned young to her.

'Good afternoon, ma'am. Sir. I'm fairly new on the force here, so that's why we won't have met before,' said the CID officer, with an easy assurance. 'I'm Detective-Inspector Richard Tomlinson, from District Headquarters. I've been told by my superior. Superintendent Mabbatt, to ascertain what's known about this unfortunate matter. I've already detailed my sergeant to assist Constable Root — one of your members, I believe — '

'He's a very nice man,' interjected Alice Godalming. 'Very considerate. I wish some of the other young fellas around were as polite.'

' — ah, quite, ma'am. Sergeant Strapp is aware of his competence, I'm sure. But Constable Root should have back-up just now. Mr. Church, you were saying?'

Church breathed a sigh. A competent

and socially acceptable policeman. Something was going right, for once. 'Forgetting myself, Inspector. Now, this lady is Mrs. Godalming — a drink, Inspector?'

Then they all heard a vast shout: 'Summers! Where's that bloody cart, man! We've got to see Arthur Root!'

The socialising was over. The offered drink was forgotten.

Tomlinson, an acute observer of humankind, had been forewarned about the plod. Clever, he'd been advised. 'And a bit more. Clever for a beat copper, Root. You'll find out.'

4

'So what happens when your mates get here, Arthur?' Gary wanted to know, as two plainclothes officers came at a steady pace along the light rough on the left of the fairway.

'You say nowt. Do what they teach you in the army. Hold your water.'

'All I want is to get off home,' said Owen Burroughs.

So do we all, Root concurred silently as Sergeant Isaac Strapp puffed up the rise to Anglers Kop. The lithe female officer with him looked as if she should be in a gym-slip. When he had outlined the nature of the find, and who had made it, Strapp made sure he had got the details right.

'And this is, again?'

'A friend, Gray Brand. He saw and heard no more than I did. And this here's the driver of the JCB. Not too good yet, are you, Owen?'

Strapp was examining the remains. 'You feeling all right?'

This was to his fellow-officer. 'I've seen a corpse before, Sergeant. I'll do,' she said firmly, moving forward a half-pace.

'Skin's just bits of leather,' said Strapp. He turned to the still-trembling finder, but addressed Root. 'I just want the basics, Constable. What have we got, for a start?'

Root indicated the area sloping away from the seventeenth tee, in the direction of the woods below; and then to the newly acquired land.

'See down there? That's the practice ground. There's an extension in hand. This hill's being levelled. So the earth-moving vehicle's here. You can see what's turned up.'

'Turned up is right. Obviously human. And old. Well?'

'It's a chance discovery. Owen here stopped his digger-blade a few feet from the remains.'

'Full name, sir?'

'Owen Burroughs, what of it? I'm just the poor sodding driver and I want out of this soon as — '

'In a minute or two, sir, please. I won't keep you long, I promise.'

He nodded for Root to continue.

'Short, Arthur. This is only the start, you know.'

* * *

They waited under the broad portico. Six pillars supported a severe classical portico. Nervously, the Secretary lit a cigarette. 'We can smoke inside, but I don't, usually. Matches, lighter, damn. Major?'

'Join you. Inspector? No? I like the Dutch cigars. Willems. Bliss keeps them for a few of us. Does it take this long to get a bloody battery changed?'

'Damned gout,' he told Tomlinson. 'So you're what, the Johnnie in charge, what d'you call it. Site Manager, something like that?'

'Usually, we'd say Crime Scene Manager, Major, and yes.' Tomlinson went on quickly, 'yes, Mr. Church. I appreciate the fact that we've not established that a crime has been committed. Just keeping your Captain in the picture, sir.'

He remembered Mabbat's advice and rechecked. 'We'll need to talk to your greenkeeper, sir. Has he been sent for?'

He had. Necessarily, this. Birtwhistle would know more about the lie of the land than any member possibly could.

Church muttered, 'I should have brought a raincoat. I can't say I'm looking forward to this, not at all. Won't the, er, the remains get wet?'

The CID inspector took it in his stride.

'We'll arrange to have them covered shortly, sir. By the way, I gather that you've not long since had another fatality here at the club.'

'Sheer bloody murder! Bad business, yes, right, Phil?'

'Ghastly!' said Phil Church. 'Three years ago it was, and my nerves were shattered for months, had to lay off the gin and down tranquillizers.'

There was a growl and a hiss of pain from the Major.

'Steer round the bloody dips, man!'

Tomlinson did not offer sympathy as they made their way fairly smoothly down the eighteenth and then up again; and less smoothly off the fairway to the excavation. 'We'll have the media types here soon. Tarts from the telly, they're the worst,' came another growl. 'Right, Phil?'

'We'll keep them in hand for you, sir. I have express orders on that point.' Straight from the top, that had become clear. 'Right here, Mr. Summers, that's close enough. Now, I'd like you all to have a good look at the remains and this Kop, then please stay beside the buggy, gentlemen, will you?'

Tomlinson motioned to his CID colleagues and Root.

'Right, we'll have the run down soon. First, who's who?'

Summers thoughtfully produced umbrellas as the rain began to lash the thin poor soil. The clenched fingers of the skeletal hand shone white, cleansed by the driven rain, as the three men advanced to the beginning of the area Root had designated as the discovery site. The skull glistened. A flap of skin fell away from the left cheekbone. Seconds passed. A minute.

'The buggy?' suggested Tomlinson.

'Gladly,' Church agreed. 'The way that arm's sticking out of the ground. Fingers — ! As if they're pointing! Horrible! What a way to end up!'

Tomlinson spoke briefly to his sergeant and DC Amy Briggs, then he asked Arthur Root to fill him in on what he knew. Like Izzy Strapp, he asked for a short briefing. 'You'll stay, Sergeant,' he ordered. 'Keeping dry?'

'And you gentlemen,' Tomlinson went on, 'before you go back to the clubhouse, what can you tell me about this matter? Anything come to mind immediately? Mr. Summers, you first, please.'

Summers shook his head. He explained that he had been appointed only in the late spring, and he could think of nothing that the inspector wasn't already aware of. Neither the major nor Church had anything to add, except for an expression of regret at the passing of a life. The Secretary had paled noticeably. He indicated that the big man beside him would speak for both.

'Had enough? Up you get then, Phil,' Major Wynne-Fitzpatrick ordered.

42

'Shocking sight. Don't blame yourself. Never get used to it.'

He cursed his gout and continued.

'Not much for you, Inspector. Can't help with an identification. Could be anyone. It's over to you, really. As for this hill we're having levelled, we've only got rumours, ancient tales, just a fog, like any old battle story, none of it substantiated. Can't really say any more that will help, so we'll get ourselves off,' the Captain grunted as he heaved himself onto the golf-buggy. 'As Phil here says, there's a mystery of sorts about the Kop. We'll have a natter in the bar when he's come round a bit. How about the JCB driver? Take him back with us? Looks all in.'

'He's needed here, sir. Now, I'll be here for quite a while, but please remain in the clubhouse. Anything you can tell me later will be of use in our investigation, so perhaps you'll review what you've seen? This officer will go with you. She'll answer any questions you might have in the meanwhile. Oh, leave me an umbrella, will you, Mr. Summers?'

The golf-buggy slid away. Root wondered if he himself would ever find himself in need of one. He glanced at Gary. The lad was holding up well. Soon, the back-up vehicles would arrive. And very soon he would have to make his initial report; just as soon as Izzy Strapp was done with.

'Constable?'

'I've started the log, sir. All down in my notebook.'

There was no hint of approval. Police training was comprehensive. Good, ordinary coppering. 'Don't give it to me verbatim. Just the basics, for now.'

So he got them, such as they were.

Arthur Root gave a time and a place, sixteen forty-three hours, those present, himself alerted by a form of distress signal, three whoops on the JCB's air-horn. Unemotionally, he detailed what he saw, what action he had taken. There was a skull, entirely visible above recently-turned soil, together with what were obviously the remains of a human arm. And so on. Three minutes, no more, he judged. 'And, after ensuring that the said vehicle was in a safe state, and ascertaining that no medical attention was needed immediately,' he finished, 'I completed my notes, sir.'

'Clear enough,' said Tomlinson. 'Sergeant? Anything to add?'

'Just normal procedure, Inspector. The constable had it all in hand. Not much for me to do, really. Wait, that's all.'

Tomlinson turned, splashing Root with the cold rain on the bright umbrella. 'Now, Mr. Burroughs. Just tell me what you did, why you're here and what you saw. Please?'

It took no more than a few minutes to have the facts confirmed by the driver. Less, for Gary. Both would make more than adequate witnesses at the inquest. Tomlinson referred again to the two officers, then declared that both Gary and Burroughs might go to the clubhouse, there to record a statement.

'If I have to,' said Owen Burroughs. 'Then I want out of here. I'm not touching that JCB either. It can stay where it is for me.'

It would, whatever his preferences. Or

those of his employer.

'Well, get along, man. Meanwhile,' he said to Arthur Root, 'You're the one with the local knowledge. No one gets under a heap of soil by choice. So, who is he, how did he get there? And did he fall into a hole, or did someone help him into it. Any ideas?'

Identification was the first issue, as Wynne-Fitzpatrick had pointed out. All stemmed from that. Who, indeed, was he?

'I can't say anything about who he was, sir. It's got to be something to do with the metal-detector, of course. They're only used by amateurs for one thing, and that's for finding old artefacts, preferably valuable. So the Kop's got to be in it, but like Mr. Church told you, it will be just guesswork. Mr. Joshua Jowett's the expert.'

'And I'm told he's made himself scarce. Root. We'll leave that for now. Let's get back to your own area of expertise. Golf, say. Coincidence doesn't exist, so it has to. Where's the link, do you suppose?'

The rain spattered musically on the taut bright yellow nylon.

'I'd be whistling in the dark, sir. Comes back to the basics, I'd say.'

Tomlinson stooped over the skull, careful to keep clear of the adjacent ground. 'Male, old, a big frame,' he said, and, echoing Root's thoughts, 'but who, that's the thing. Never come across anything quite like this.'

Vehicles arrived, several of them. All but one made for the car park, and then were lost to sight from the Kop. A flashy little MG, that would be the Home Office pathologist, Dr. Jane Anderson, come to tell them that the punter in the rain was most definitely dead, Tomlinson noted. A Crime Scene van followed, then a blue Transit with a contingent of detectives, likely briefed already to start the inter-views; and, in a big SUV came the man himself.

'Well,' said Inspector Tomlinson. 'Company.'

He got up, to find Strapp indicating the progress of a dark blue Landcruiser as it made its noisy way towards them. Permission must have been given for the intrusion, thought Root. It was full, mostly with large male bodies, two in blue. It was not a decorous easy-paced trundle by an almost silent buggy: the blue patrol four-track thumped over rough ground alongside the eighteenth with panache.

Arthur Root felt a sense of *déjá vu*. The back-up Tomlinson had sent for. Uniformed constabulary would take over his duties. And he was back with Mabbatt.

'Can't be,' said Strapp, squinting through the rain. 'In the front, sir. Not the Super is it?'

Root knew that he would not have a great deal of contact now with the investigatory proceedings: the CID inspector had got all he needed. Maybe the evening meal would not be too far gone in Ursula's new Bosch oven. Waiting around was over. The wheels had turned. A bit late, a bit slowly, but things would move fast now. He knew who, and what, was coming.

'Well, now,' said Tomlinson. 'Surprise, surprise.'

* * *

'Saw your bike out in the rain,' Josie told Gary Brand. 'Nice bike. You got the Lycra gear? Bet you look good when you're racing. I put it in Fred's shed, the wooden one. Want to see it's all right?'

From the kitchen window, Bliss watched her vanish with the tall young man. 'Oh, you bitch,' he said.

'So why haven't I met you before?' asked Gary.

'What I was asking myself,' Josie told him, drawing the creaking old door close. 'I can't stay long. Charlie's always on the lookout. You're not engaged or going regular, or owt?'

Gary knew that whatever answer he formulated, it wouldn't much matter, not right now. The girl was firm and pliable at once; well-rounded but with taut muscle beneath. He put his arms round her and looked down into dark blue eyes that picked out a reflection of the bar of grey light where the door was slightly ajar. Tensions and flickers of violent flashbacks vanished. 'Over here,' he whispered, drawing her to a darker corner.

'Oh, Gary,' she said, 'we can't be doing

this, not right away, can we? Not so soon, love?'

In the same moment, they weren't. A loud incoherent shout broke the quiet of the interior, with its heavy smells of cut grass and oil and its aura of secrecy and remoteness from the solid conservative Wolvers milieu:

'You mad bastard! You can keep your sodding job!'

The door was flung back, and a figure staggered halfway through the doorway. Gary's firm arms tightened. 'Keep quiet, Josie,' she heard him whisper. 'The JCB driver's getting slagged off. We leave it alone. Not our problem. I've had my say to the police. I'm out of it.'

* * *

Owen Burroughs recovered himself and faced his boss in the car park. He had been summarily sacked, after a bawling out that left him at first bewildered and then fiercely indignant.

'You're telling me what, you bastard!' he yelled. 'Just plough the poor sod back

50

into his grave — you mean, just go on with levelling the Kop and shove him down a few feet under, like!'

That was exactly what Knight had meant.

'It could have been a few old bones from years back — it could have been an old dog or a few pigs they'd buried with swine-fever, for all you know, you bleeding Welsh git! Why couldn't you just do what you're paid for, not get me into a shit of a mess with the law! They've cordoned off the whole damned site, and I'm buggered if I'm keeping you on a minute longer! Just get off before I — '

That was when small, but thickset Owen Burroughs realised that seven years of labouring in the depot had just gone up in smoke. He'd signed up with Knight when he had come along to buy the ill-run business for peanuts. So far he'd shown acumen and kept the competent employees on. Owen went with the site. Now, he was out of it.

'Pick up your envelope in the morning,' Knight told him, quietly, but hard. 'And don't think of making waves. Ever. You got that?'

At a safe distance, Owen Burroughs yelled:

'You're not right in the 'ead, you know that? You don't act like — '

He stopped. There was no going back, not with such venom in the man. Out. Owen looked down at his wide, calloused hands. There was still strength in them. Maybe there was work Swansea way.

'Me, I'm gone!'

Listening at one of his many sounding boards, the steward smiled. The members and clientele, the paid help and the chance drop-ins: all their misfortunes nourished him, and more than made up for low pay and unending faux-subservience. And now that the coppers were involved, things were stewing nicely. Voices, low but young and passionate, vibrated around the old cupboard, long forgotten, never opened in half a century, where he accreted fragments of lives.

★　★　★

Josie Marsden said it for both of them.

'I'm not in the mood any more, Gary. I hate all this kind of thing. That boss of his must be a real hard case. I heered too many of his kind on a rough night at the bar. Poor old bloke. Outed, just like that. My dad never got over being kicked out when the pits around here closed. Will I see you again?'

'Count on it.'

The day had closed in. So had the all-too-omnipresent echoes of fierce explosions, shrieks of pain and blackening blood as warm with insects. Gary Brand too wanted no more of violence and sudden death.

'I'm away,' he said. 'Got to be.'

5

The impact of Superintendent Mabbat's arrival was immediate.

Tomlinson's polite gesture was at once rebuffed. 'No, I don't want a bloody umbrella! What am I, the sugar-plum fairy?'

Superintendent Mabbatt shifted his big frame through the wide, high door. He was light enough on his feet once clear of the car, though his bulk had increased considerably since his last appearance on a Wolvers fairway. Still drinking then, Arthur Root judged, as the big head swivelled around to where he waited.

'Bloody hell, Root, how d'you do it? It's not ten minutes since you found that golfer, whatsisname Tom-something, got his golf stick banged into his brains. Now you've found another one! And you were at the golf again, were you? Millionaire's life, that right?'

Arthur Root restrained a break in his

thin, sun-reddened cheeks. It would not do to smile, not given the Superintendent's views on the pursuit of all sensible men. 'Golf again, Root?'

Mabbatt had had to go easy on his legendary dislikes. He no longer castigated queers, Socialists, Pakis, voyeurs, his virago of a wife, immigrants, the Met, Chinese takeaways, women police officers, and silly buggers who paid more attention to their golf-sticks than orthodox coppering and beer.

What would he make of a uniform whose wife had made it her mission to convince him that ballroom dancing, in particular one of the more showy South American styles, was a better way of filling his off-duty hours?

Do not explain, Root told himself. 'Pleasant sort of recreation, sir.'

'Not for that poor bugger,' Mabbat told him. He motioned to Tomlinson and wagged a thick finger at the skull. 'Looks intact, but you can't tell. Just another lot of bones for our forensic medico to dig out before we get anything definite. Youngish one. She'll soon come up with something. Got her like that,' he said, offering a large, spatulate and calloused palm. 'You set up for the paparazzi, then, Inspector?'

They could expect a close scrutiny very soon. Inevitably the entire local media were both alerted and Wolvers-bound. Tomlinson would act as minder until Mabbatt was ready to take them head on himself.

'In hand, sir. Going to be quite a circus. Local, but there'll be lots of interest. They'll be digging through the old files and picking out bits on the location. Angler's Kop, got a history, so Constable Root and Mr. Church have told me. And the Captain. Major Wynne-Fitzpatrick.'

'Yes. The Major.'

It was said with caution: so, like had called to like at a rarefied level.

Mabbatt was now on one knee, a searcher on a warm scent. The others caught his enthusiasm. They were intensely aware that he'd lead them well and investigate diligently, energetically and thoroughly, whatever. Toes, it had certainly been hinted.

should not be trodden on, Root was sure of it. But it was not in Mabbatt's bag, his nature, to exercise much tact. He'd unravel the mystery held in this thin, poor soil if anyone could.

'Right, lads!' he called as more personnel arrived and began to tape off the site and set up a green canvas tent on metal scaffolding. 'Let's get on with it. Now, then, Dr. Anderson, just the job for a rainy day! See you're wrapped up well, lass! Sergeant Strapp, we'll have a look round, then relieve you and Root here, and get a bite in the clubhouse. Inspector Tomlinson will stay with you, Doctor. Oh, and just one thing. My Chief would like some priority given to this one — I know you're not one to speculate, but if you can give me a quick rundown on what you can see?'

'No.'

It silenced Mabbatt. The young woman was tall, thin, quite composed, and evidently used to officious senior detectives. Her stylish pink metal-framed spectacles were blurred: behind them, dark eyes regarded him stonily. She hefted a small case and adjusted her long bright-pink waterproof. 'The time is eighteen o-six hours. Today is Monday, September the sixteenth,' she informed a small recorder. 'The remains that are visible are human. They comprise of a skull, and a forearm and hand.' Root listened carefully as she described the scene and detailed her intentions. 'The remains are in an advanced stage of decomposition. I am about to commence the exhumation.' She broke off. 'And quite soon, Superintendent, I may be able to give you a preliminary report.'

Mabbatt smiled. He had almost misjudged her, he told himself. Maybe her inexperience had caused her to be apprehensive of him at first, whereas she was distinctly helpful now. And had he challenged that sharp denial of hers? Of course not. He congratulated himself on his forebearance — he had shown tact, one more example of his intrapersonal abilities. Time to move on.

Mabbatt was enjoying himself thoroughly.

'Root, you're on!'

Phil Church and the professional took Amy Briggs to where the greenkeeper waited. Freddie Birtwhistle had steadfastly refused to enter the clubhouse. He would not leave his dog.

'You all right, sir? Course you are. You'll be the head greenkeeper here at Wolvers,' said Amy Briggs. 'Mr. Birtwhistle, aren't you?' she asked Fred, who wouldn't look at her.

'She come about these gippo kids, then?'

'No, Fred,' said Summers. 'It's what the lad told you. At the Kop — the skeleton. Turned up by the JCB just now.'

'Don't know about that. Driver's job, not mine. Told to keep out of it, aren't I, till he's done.'

Amy Briggs interrupted:

'We'll have some questions for you, but not just now, Mr. Birtwhistle.'

'Don't know why 'Itler didn't go for 'im.'

A huge, gaunt old greyhound peered out of the plastic sidepiece. It opened a wide mouth, full of glistening white teeth and snarled at Amy Briggs. She showed bright white teeth at him.

'Go for who, Mr. Birtwhistle?'

'Gippo kid, like. Not skeleton, luv!'

Fred pulled thick-lensed spectacles off his nose and drank heavily-sweetened tea from an old pint-sized chipped mug. He said that t'old dog needed feeding: however, he was told firmly that his presence would be required here for at least another hour. Or two.

'Read me paper, then,' he said, settling himself onto the seat of the big red Fordson. 'If tha wants to pay me for nowt, ain't my lookout.'

* * *

They were established in the bar.

Back down the seventeenth, the rain drummed down on the faded green canvas and the half-dozen of forensic investigators. Mabbatt felt that life was good. His interactive abilities were non-pareil in South Yorkshire coppering.

'God, you're talking as if there's been

some kind of horrible crime done here, Superintendent!'

Mabbatt had reintroduced himself to those of the Committee he had met before and told the major he was honoured, then said.

'A crime, Mr. Church? No one's said anything about a crime having being committed.' Mabbatt did not pause long enough for the Secretary to end the sentence: 'yet'. 'No, all we've got so far is an unexplained death.'

'On the Kop,' said the huge, burly Captain, who overtopped even Mabbatt by a handspan or more. 'Our land now, so we're all involved. Had a word with Alice here, Mrs. Godalming. Knows a bit about the law, you know.'

Mabbatt did. He had found her a most formidable magistrate, not at all liberal minded. 'Had the pleasure, Major,' he said. 'Look forward to anything the lady has to say, gentlemen. Oh, there is one more thing I'll need your help with, by the way. It's most important at the beginning of any inquiry to get down what facts we can right away. Whilst it's fresh in everyone's minds?'

He explained that, much as he appreciated the co-operation and forethought shown so far, Mr. Church would readily understand that he would need a base. Somewhere central and private. 'Is there somewhere I can use, Mr. Church?'

Church knew it was coming.

'I'll need my office,' said Church heavily, 'so I suppose it'll have to be the billiards room. It's just opposite the members' bar-lounge. As you know, Superintendent. You can ring for tea, coffee, what you like. The steward's an inquisitive wretch, but he's good at his job. I'll arrange it. I suppose, sandwiches?'

Mabbatt was enjoying himself thoroughly.

'I recall the ham was very good, sir. Yes, I expect the lads could do with a bite. It's going to be a longish session for all of us. But we'll get there, that's what we do. This could be serious. You did say you were all right?'

Alice Godalming was vastly intrigued.

The huge police officer, square as a

T34, had gone. Ted was not yet back and she could listen to the way the small details began to fill the gaps.

Major Wynne-Fitzpatrick said that they'd have to fend English Heritage off before they got seriously interested. 'All bosh about a battle around that bit of a hill,' he said. 'Nothing to defend, you see, Alice,' his sole companion in the vast oak-panelled room, for Church had taken himself off to berate Bliss, 'nothing of strategic value, and who'd choose to make a stand for nothing at all? At least at Spion Kop our staff thought they had an objective. Found themselves badly exposed as it turned out. Got the, ah, stuffing knocked out of them by the Boers' gunners, but it went down as a gallant action. Kop, indeed. Wonder who wished the name on that pimple?'

'Who indeed, Major.'

'JJ would know. Our Mr. Chips. Clubbable sort of fellow, but perhaps a bit of an oddball, eh, Alice?'

'He's a very private sort of person, so my Ted always says, but we've always found him an excellent companion, even if he does concentrate on just one or two topics. That's Ted's estimation and he's a good judge of character. As for his local expertise. I expect Superintendent Mabbatt will get round to that in due course, Alfred.'

'Yes sure you're right. Been told he's rough around the edges, but still a dogged one. We need drinks. Bliss! Brandy, Alice, yes? Yes, you need one.'

The major was more a Mark V Tiger, she thought. Why object?

* * *

Mabbatt was engaged in a mild form of browbeating, which did not seem to be having its desired effect. He had perused his memories of Constable Root whilst taking advantage of Wolvers' impressive toilet facilities. Aftershave at one's disposal. *Pour L 'Homme.* Fancy.

Root he'd said to himself as he splashed it on liberally, bit of a burr, that one. But, Joseph Mabbatt, you are famed for your intra-personnel skills.

Everyone admitted it. Downright and straightforward and bluff, but with a profound knowledge of human nature, that was how Mabbatt knew he was seen. Yorkshire through and through and proud of it, and a beacon to all in his command: they may at times have feared him, but they respected him — and with that respect came a sincere admiration, even a measure of devotion.

'I'm lucky,' he said to his reflection in the mirror above the washbowl. 'Born to lead. I could be a Roman.'

By the time he got back to the impromptu incident room, sandwiches had arrived, and Root had had the foresight to order beer for them both. Tomlinson was still at the diggings, of course, and would be until he had escorted the remains to the mortuary with the pathologist. Strapp and that young lass — good figure — were looking after the staff, getting an overview, keeping them safely herded away from one another; whilst he, Mabbatt, would glean what he could from Root. He wanted a few minutes with this problematical plod, who was doing too much cogitating for a uniform.

Give me a rundown on the people at this toffee-nosed club, he'd told him. And it was taking too long, since the first pint was low in the glass and most of the well-garnished platter of sandwiches was gone too. 'Yes, two more, love,' he called to Josie as she peered into the billiards room. 'Just a half for the constable, though. He'll be driving. In your own car, aren't you, Root? Now, what have you got to tell me?'

Root recognised the technique. Mabbatt couldn't help using disorienting questions even when he was addressing one of his own.

'Yes, sir, I'm driving. And I've got to remind myself that this is a bit of a facer altogether, this discovery. For the committee, I mean. And the rest of the members and staff, of course. But it puts a lot of strain on those at the top, and it's not as if they're young any longer. All over seventy.'

'They look well enough, bar a game leg

66

and too many gins — hale enough, especially Her Honour. Alice Godalming was hard on violence, I recollect. Come on, they're not your mates! You don't have friends when you go coppering. They might be highly respectable members here and you might be one of them, but you're the law first and last, remember. Right?'

'Of course, sir.'

'Tell you what, the staff, then. Start with them, yes? Who knows what, you know how it goes, happens everywhere, who's got it in for some other bugger. Soon get to the bottom of it.'

Cynical, but right. As always, thought Root, you talk to the people who watched and listened, especially those best placed for acquiring bits of information and weaving them into a verifiable tapestry.

'The pro, Mick Summers, him first, sir. He's got to know every inch of the course, that's how he makes his living. He's personable enough, popular too. It's only natural he hears a lot. Likes to make a splash, though. He's spending beyond his resources.'

'Single?'

'Divorcing, I hear, sir. The ladies like him, before he ditches them. Latest one he's taken off the shelf he should worry about. Angela Knight, that's the ex-wife of Terry Knight who's contributed Owen Burroughs and the JCB to try to get full membership, which he won't. She'll see to it. She's been a member here for years and detests him. All a bit complicated, sir.'

'Don't go into it all just now. Who else?'

Root told him that Charlie Bliss was still listening and storing up indiscretions, always to reinforce his position at Wolvers. When he added that the steward had made a mistake in getting Josie Marsden in, Mabbatt grinned happily. 'Can't blame the fat little creep for trying, can we? Next? And try to get back to those bones, will you?'

Root explained the background to the purchase of the farmland adjoining the Wolvers acres. This brought him to Freddie Birtwhistle, who had not been enthusiastic about the extension. He thought the soil poor and the possibility of subsidence a real one, given the proximity of the river and the unknown factor of old workings, burrowings going back hundreds if not thousands of years. 'The Greens Committee and to some extent Mick Summers tell him what's required in a general way, but it's him that keeps the course in good order. He's been here most of his working life. He knows every blade of grass, every grain of sand in the bunkers, how much water's left in the pond by the third, and what sort of turf to use on the extension — what was Anglers Kop. He's still waiting in his tractor cab with his old dog, by the way, sir.'

'He'll keep.'

Mabbatt glanced at his watch. Surely prim pink-specs had done enough digging by now? He knew he wouldn't settle till he had something to work on. For instance, what Strapp had come out with: did someone help the deceased into that little old hill that was supposed to have its own bit of history, or what? And what about that historical connection, then? He reminded himself that this reluctant witness, aka Mr. Chips, was yet to be questioned. Tactfully.

'Right, I'm nearly done, for now.' So were the sandwiches and beer.

'I'll talk to your bigwigs here next. But put me in the picture about this one they call 'Mister — Chips'? Where the sodding hell did they get that from? But get that blonde lass to bring another pint fast, will you?'

Root had passed up the ham sandwiches. He was envisaging his waiting meal at home. He waited calmly for the Superintendent of detectives to continue, which, after a grunt of satisfaction, he did.

'Told this Mr. Chips is an eccentric. Obsessional about this hobby of his. Canny, though. Had the sense to scarper before we got here, right? Can't be that addled, Root. Go on.'

Mabbatt's special intonation indicated that he had reservations about the mental condition of Root's fellow-member, informant and friend. And did he live on some other sodding planet, not this chunk of formerly industrial South Yorkshire? But discretion won, and it didn't take long to give Josh Jowett's history, as known to Wolvers' one constabulary member of the lowest level in the hierarchy of the force. And JJ's views on history, as they applied to the matter of the Spion Kop mystery. Root settled the unstated query about his psychological competence at once.

'He's in possession of a complete set of marbles, is Mr. Josh Jowett, sir, and he's more than a hobbyist. He's an enthusiastic amateur archaeologist very knowledgeable. Retired from teaching, not local, some public school, classics master in the old mould, a real-life Mr. Chips. We're friendly, to a point. I wouldn't say he's lively company, but he's always interesting. Takes the *Guardian*, sir,' said Root slyly, and giving time for a snort of disdain, which didn't form, so he went on, 'I've given him a lift here when his car's been in dock, and I've also taken him home a time or two when he's forgotten how many gins he's got down, then we've talked, or at least he has. You can guess what about.'

'Bloody well enlighten me. And not sociology rubbish. This Kop, keep to that, Root. Romans and all. What's his interest, where's he from with these old stories?'

Arthur Root could feel that his own usefulness was coming to an end. For him, the investigation was nearly over. Brisk young detectives would ferret out what was left to find: they'd explore the ruin of the Cartwrights' derelict farm buildings, comb-search the excavation once the sad old bones were bagged and removed; and bedevil amiable old JJ unmercifully for days. And he'd be out of it. Not, he thought, that he could do much more: chance, though, would be a fine thing.

'Well, sir, he gives the legends no credence at all. Dismisses them all out of hand. Takes the stand that they're in the realms of mythology, even. Mr. Jowett is firm that the Kop isn't the site of some Romano-Briton conflict — that's how he puts it, by the way — it's just a handy location for a build-up of folklore and flummery.'

Mabbatt wanted to know more.

'Always some basis in a rumour. Nowt comes from nowt. You know that well enough. Tittle-tattle, whispers, downright lies. They all add up. Well?'

'Josh — Mr. Jowett — would go for downright lies, sir. He's against the kind of vogue that romanticised the Middle Ages in the nineteenth century. You'll remember the folly, sir, by the car park?'

Mabbatt nodded. 'What's that got to do with it?'

Briefly, Root told him about the old iron-master's effete son, the Romantic. 'He got through a good part of the old man's wealth. He spent quite a lot of his inheritance in dreaming up recreations of the past. The folly was only a start.'

The folly, a pleasant enough whim of the ironmaster's son who read Tennyson and had long, blonde hair, had been created by the simple expedient of ordering his workforce to demolish a couple of old cottages, evicting the farmworkers instanter. There was a full history of the family in the club's library, so Josh Jowett had told Root and those of the members who would listen to him for more than a couple of minutes at a time.

'So you're a bit of romantic yourself, Root?'

'Not really, sir. But the history of these parts has its relevance to the Kop, and that's where the bones are being disinterred, and that's what you wanted me to elaborate on, and the folly leads on to it. Shall I go on?'

It was agreed, a briefer nod signifying so.

'Well, sir.'

Long and early dead Jeremy Saunders-Roe identified with Millais' works, in particular his *Ophelia* and often thought a watery death would become him. And his physician recorded duly that he had so died. Pneumonia, that was close enough, to the son's prognostication, Root went on.

'Form of drowning, isn't it?'

'A known fact. Matters, does it? Lost me now, Root. And?'

'Well, Jeremy's ideas got wilder. He looked up, or rather got a couple of hired historians from his old Oxford college to look up, the old tales about the Coritani

— locals, sir. Not a particularly warlike tribe, but they took it hard when the Romans came by on their way to York to thrash the Brigantes. Jeremy was very taken with the notion of the Coritani as a noble breed pushed to the limit. He identified with them, I expect. The hired experts gave him what he wanted, with a full-scale Fort Alamo-style last stand on the Kop — sir?'

Mabbatt looked around him with something approaching dislike for the elegant drawing room. Oils and faded photographs were ranged around the thickly-embossed walls. A large modern painting was lit by a small beam of light; a golfer holding a golf-stick up in triumph: an Asiatic. Jap, likely. 'Kop, that's South Africa.'

Kop? California? Japs?

Root was rambling. Or maybe not. Say nowt. Yet.

'Josh Jowett's got it all at his fingertips, sir. I expect you'll want his version?' And before his superior could respond, he went on quickly, 'It's better to catch him when he's had a good sleep.'

And that, Arthur Root reflected soon afterwards, was that. Mabbatt had regarded him sourly, thanked him for his contribution to the investigation and told him that he might well be of farther assistance, though his tone suggested it was unlikely. He checked with lzzy Strapp that Gary could go home, and then made for his ageing Megane. It had been a disturbing experience. Home beckoned, and he was glad when he merged with the early evening traffic for No 27 and Ursula's relieved chiding. As he left the quiet of the billiards room, with its hint of brandy and cigar smoke, Amy Briggs stopped him.

'Arthur? Hang on, will you a minute,' she said. 'It's 'Itler, like. Your greenkeeper's fretting about his dog's dinner. Is Mr. Mabbatt free now?'

Arthur Root didn't await the outcome.

★ ★ ★

'What's up, then?' Mabbatt asked.

The old man with the huge, gaunt dog on his lap didn't appear to have heard. He was peering closely at a tabloid newspaper.

Phil Church and the major had accompanied Mabbatt and Amy Briggs to where the red John Deere was parked, alongside the greens equipment shed. On the way, the Secretary had given him a brief biography. A dedicated employee, brilliant with the greens, but of an obdurate nature, that was Freddie Birtwhistle. His skills were prized, though his future at Wolvers was problematical, should he not take the opthalmological advice he had been given. 'Fred's due for his cataracts done, right, Major? He won't go, though. Makes it difficult here.'

'Be blind in a year or two,' the major added. 'Just can't bear the notion of cutting new eyes-holes in his head. Can't say I do either, Superintendent. Fred, Mr. Mabbatt wants a word. Then that beast of yours can get at his food.'

They both stared back balefully.

'Just bloody greenkeeper, aren't I? And 'e keeps the buggers away!'

Mabbatt glared, and the dog was first to break eye-contact.

'Doing his job. Nothing wrong with that, Fred. Now our officers have put you in the picture, I know that. So what have you got to tell us?'

'The remains at the Kop?' prompted DC Briggs. 'Like we told you just a bit ago.' She mouthed an 'excuse me, sir', which brought a nod from Mabbat. 'You can tell Mr. Mabbatt here.'

Fred Birtwhistle shifted the dog and the tabloid aside and wiped his thick spectacles. 'I don't know nowt I haven't told sergeant here and the lass. Out through woods down by river when I were 'aving me snap by t'old gate that broke. After the scrap from the Cartwright farm, that's what. Couldn't work out 'ow they got past 'Itler in one piece, like. Not right off. But I seed cheeky little sod, one with that gippo gold medal they wear round their scrawny necks, he bamboozles 'Itler 'ere and gives 'im a kiss on nose. Any other bugger, 'e'd 'ave 'ad 'is throat out.'

Mabbatt stared at the wizened face and the red-rimmed eyes for a moment. 'We'll get one of the officers to take it down, then you can go.'

He did not trouble to avoid the streaming rain as he headed for the entrance to the clubhouse,

Alice Godalming and Ted Jones were about to make their departure.

'Not very forthcoming, our Fred, Superintendent?'

'It's all grist, ma'am. Good evening to you both.'

Major Wynne-Fitzpatrick thought they should adjourn to the bar. He glanced out of the big bay window once they were comfortable. 'Very odd business,' he said to Mabbatt. 'Still, your inspector's got it all in hand, I see. Minimal collateral damage from the press and such-like — good show, Superintendent. It's much appreciated. A beer is it? Stones's, Bliss. A pint, of course, man! Mr. Mabbatt's had a hard day! Keeps it well, so he does, Charlie Bliss. Good head on it.'

* * *

Root waved a salute to the officers at the front of Wolvers, then he drove out onto the drive proper, with the well-grown sycamores at decent intervals all the three-quarter mile long way between the fairways. He took at quick look in the rear-view mirror at a sight that invariably thrilled. It might be a symbol of capitalism and repression, it certainly was built on the sweat and early deaths of so many viciously-worked Yorkshire folk; but there it was, the towering bulk of the iron-master's splendid mansion, topped by a union flag that fluttered hesitantly in a slight breeze, bright and challenging against a sky itself like iron. And himself, an unlikely heir to it all. Past the one-time lodge keeper's single-storied, mullion-windowed he drove, not fast, watchful and shamefully proud, past what were now Fred's fading rhododendron bushes, where 'Itler ruled by night. Grey old stone walls slid by, all under the iron sky.

Then he was out on the road back to Gritmarsh, a hungry man, but a somewhat disconsolate police officer. The detective's life, where you got to see the end of the story mostly, had never drawn him; regular police work had. And yet.

Back, Arthur Root told himself, to your own patch. Regular coppering. Maybe he'd get a secondhand look at the unfolding story. Maybe.

★   ★   ★

Tomlinson was occupied with fending off the reporters' fairly polite but insistent clamour. 'So he was golfing or was he looking for Saxon loot when he got clobbered?' called one heavily made-up older journalist. 'Did someone belt him with a niblick, like the last one that got topped here? Or did he get it with his metal-detector? Anyway, who is he? Is he old? Has he got his bus pass on him?'

Two colleagues decided that she had struck the right note.

Tomlinson showed them the printout he had just cobbled together. 'Lily,' he said, 'and you two gentlemen, thank you for your attendance. This is what I can tell you right now, and it's all you're getting. Here it is.' And he read, quite slowly, 'The remains of a person unknown as yet have been discovered in the grounds of Wolvers

81

Golf Club. We are treating the matter as an unexplained incident and have therefore sealed the scene for forensic examination. You can quote — '

'Scene?' snapped Lily Ogg, who worked for the regional group of newspapers that covered most of South Yorkshire. 'So we're looking at a crime scene. Tommo? Was the head bashed about? Found a weapon yet? A bloke is it, a golfer did you say? I can quote you on that — '

Tomlinson held up his hands. 'You are a trier, Lily, my love. But you do rabbit on, don't you? Now listen, when the Super's assessed all the intelligence available, I've no doubt he'll be delighted to let you in on what he's got. Mr. Mabbatt is famous for his respect for the media, especially your esteemed traditional part of it. He has instructed me to cooperate with you fully. Meanwhile, please, as they say, leave the premises, my dear.'

'You're a lovely talker,' Lily told him. 'I could fancy you. Ring me?'

'Get her,' said the young man with the camcorder. 'Good try, Lily.'

Breakfast was always a hectic affair in the Root household. For one thing, there were diets to be considered and preferences expressed, which could change daily. Tom was firm for eggs and bacon: like his dad, he insisted; and again Root, as he contemplated the big teapot, had a momentary tremor of doubt as he thought of his son, a probationer out on his first night patrol. 'You don't always have to do what I do,' he said gruffly, as Ursula brought in two sizeable plates, one with mushrooms, the other with Root's favourite plum tomatoes.

The twins wandered through without speaking.

'Teeth?' enquired Ursula.

'After brekkie?' said Hattie.

'Mum?'

'This time all right, Sarah. Hot breakfast, you two? Bacon?'

They shook their heads and reached for a heady mix of cereal and dried fruit. 'Yoggi, Mum?' said Sarah.

'Not bacon,' confirmed Hattie. 'Uggh.'

'You're on the ball, lookalikes,' Beth approved. 'See. It's just dead greasy fatty pig. I mean, our Tom, and you Dad as well, just think of the cholesterol you're shoving down your throat, you two! Eh, Dad, was that a snout that left the message, the one I picked up when I went for my run?'

Dead pigs. *Snout. Got it.* Beth had Ursula's flair for associating the wildly disassociative. 'You're not supposed to take my messages, lass, you know that quite well. It's police business.'

She wouldn't be put down.

'Mrs. O'Brien left another today. She said she saw that little kid that got through the side window, the one at the cellar top, and it must have been shut for forty years, Dad, and he'd have to be a right shrimp, wouldn't he?'

'Beth! It's supposed to be confidential, love.'

The twins grabbed toast and orange juice, then ran upstairs, squealing.

'You've got to go to the station, Arthur,' said Ursula. 'Sergeant Brown said to go.'

The remains, of course.

'Dad, was he looking for treasure?' said

Tom earnestly. 'Had to be, Gary says. No reason for the gear otherwise.'

'You've spoken to Gary? When?'

'Rang for you about seven this morning. He thought you'd told me about it. It's an old model, but pretty powerful. American-made, about fifteen, twenty years ago. A CX-Surefind, cost about seventy quid then.'

'Go on. Gary said what?'

'He'd ring when you're back from your walkabout. I told him between six and eight, O.K?'

None of it was O.K, but how could a community policeman keep secret when there was daily a small barrage of calls to be noted on what was, after all, the family communications centre. Central wouldn't give him a secure line, much less a recording machine with an encryption facility. 'For local coppering? Come on, Arthur,' he'd been told by his sergeant. 'You get a little computer to do desk work for you in a few months, though. The government's up for re-election, so they hope, and they've allocated a few million to keep you on the beat, not filling in forms and supping canteen coffee all day long.'

Brown, his sergeant, was a cheerful ex-pro soccer player, late to the trade and immensely happy with his lot. Root had slept well, though he had dreamt about strange old conflicts. What would the day bring?

It was explained to him.

'Salsa,' said Ursula. 'When you get back, we'll go over that slinky bit for me. And you put your dancing pumps on — and you, our Beth, you do not bring your street mates to look through the window and take the mickey, you hear?'

Beth would, undoubtedly. The three nubile teens who were her little gang — my lass a natural gang leader, thought Root mixedly, good or bad?

Would she go astray or lead her mates to good things? All were lively and attractive in their own particular way, one red-haired and athletic, one tiny and a fearsome fighter in her infant days, and one a tall, willowy coal-black girl with titian hair, who dreamt of swaying down a catwalk and para-gliding off Alicante. The former was to come, the latter she was skilled at, to judge by the latest video he'd watched, Shahalim O'Grady.

And then he thought of teens and kids and what they could be manouevred into trying, just for the fun of it. Buying. Being pushed. *Skunk*.

Beth wouldn't let her glimpse into police work go.

'This snout. Did you think of the name? I mean, you can't have everyone knowing what sort of a peeper or keyhole snooper he is, can you? I quite like the name. Inventive. Sort of local Gritmarsh colour.'

'Name?'

'Why, 'Mr. Chips', Dad.'

'Ursula, restrain your daughter.'

Beth wouldn't let it go. 'So what's with the snout? It's a bit enigmatic, what he said. Is it a sort of code? I mean, like a password on the internet, sort of like when you want to get into a chat room and all the blokes are kiddie-mad pervies about ninety years of age and want to meet you in the park with a bag of sweets and evil intentions?'

'Beth!'

'All right, Mum,' said her daughter, momentarily cowed. A nano-moment, though. 'Dad What do you pay him? Ten? Fifty? Or do you dish out hash and things you've taken on a raid?'

Now she was laughing. Not at him, just at her own zany take on his work. 'It's police business, love. Please leave it. And don't blab. I mean it. Especially not to your mates, you hear? It really is important. And serious.'

'Like salsa?' she said, as she left for school.

Arthur Root panicked momentarily. *Salsa.* He'd tried and tried to get the sequence just so, but Ursula wanted the right knee where the green dancing frock she'd slit and shortened salsa-style hooked enticingly round his thigh, her elegant calf horizontal to the floor with her diamante heels glistening and the line of her well-muscled calf clearly delineated for the onlookers to admire, envy and lust after. And to get me, going, Root squirmed happily. He put his teacup down.

'I'll be in the front room, Ursula. Our Beth's right. It isn't routine. CID will want to get onto it right away.'

'Yesterday? To do with that telly report, then? At the club?'

They'd watched the brief newscast when the children were all in bed. Inspector Tomlinson had looked calm and completely assured. Not bland, and in no way dismissive of the gravity of the find: exactly what Root would have expected from a suave and educated police officer of his rank. He'd said just enough to keep the listener aware that all was being done in the proper manner. The grisly find was under investigation. It was expected that the unknown deceased person would soon be identified. And here was a development, on the family BT catch-all.

'Has to be the Kop find,' said Root. 'I didn't want our lass making the connection with Josh Jowett. He's an old man, but he's sharp as a knife. She's only met him a couple of times, so calling himself 'Mr. Chips' wouldn't mean much. Best that way. I'll get onto it, love.'

It was terse, and to the point.

He had skipped the more or less routine complaints and pleas. Josh Jowett's voice was clear, if a bit halting: 'It's Mr. Chips, for Constable Root. I know who it is.'

Arthur Root was not fazed. Information came in odd ways.

Now, procedure, he told himself. Josh Jowett hadn't said much, but it was significant. So he knew the identity of the man in the Kop, did he? My duty, but not really my worry, Arthur Root told himself. There were those who were well paid and well trained for what came next. There was a fixed way of doing things. Get through to Central, for a start. Give Sergeant Brown the gist, then ask for orders. The day would have to be rescheduled, of course. Gritmarsh and Hagthorpe's problems would have to give way to what could well be a serious crime inquiry.

Sergeant Brown, first. He would take it from there.

'They'll want this, Arthur. Hang about, will you?'

Brown had quickly taken in the import

of his news and put him through to Izzy Strapp right away. 'Arthur, is it? Knew you'd be calling in.' Sergeant Isaac Strapp was expecting his call, was he? He was 'Can't hear you, Arthur. Speak up, will you?'

Root did so. 'I have a message on the answer-machine. It's related to the inquiry at Wolvers. That member you wanted. Mr. Joshua Jowett. From what I can make out, he can identify the corpse.'

Strapp let him talk first. There was no particular curiosity, no eagerness, which threw Root again. 'It's short, came in at o-seven-eleven today. It reads, 'I know who it is'.'

'That all?'

'All. Want to listen in? I think you'd make it out.'

The offer was refused. 'He knows, does your Mr. Chips? We do as well.'

★ ★ ★

'Right, then, we'll have a twirl.'

Quite mad, was Ursula.

'And we're still going to Harrogate on

91

Saturday,' he was told. 'Dad and mum are having the twins. And you want to look at the way they've done up the Royal Hall, I know that. You deserve one Saturday off a month. Arthur. And I want to do some shopping. Come on.'

She had understood at once that he had suffered a setback. And she had the wisdom to know how to change his mood. In a moment, she had the garage pulsing with the beat of a big band. And then he was holding her, heavy workaday shoes on his big feet, and it was the best thing he knew of: his wife in his arms and a long and busy day ahead. After all of six minutes, she told him that that was quite enough, and to get out and earn his pay.

So he clomped off the flooring of his own largish garage at No. 27 Acacia Avenue. He'd been lucky in getting the old flooring cheap from a re-cycler near Darfield, not too far away when they'd used an unexpected legacy from Ursula's great-aunt down in Waterlooville to move from the police-house on the main Rotherham road to this much more spacious house — three bedrooms, and a big extension put on by a jobbing builder, who'd put them right about what they could do with the place. Ursula had dumbfounded him by saying she wanted a ballroom: in the garage. She'd got it too. Root told himself admiringly. Off he'd gone in a hired van and soon it was laid and polished by yet another mate of the builder, and under an old chandelier — Scope charity shop in Sheffield — away they sailed onto the mini-ballroom floor, to the rhythm of the wild and yet amazingly languorous beat. And hilarity from Beth and her mates ever after. He smiled fondly and realised he was drifting.

He didn't know much; yet he could speculate. The deceased, for a start. Inspector Tomlinson had told him to call in for an update when he himself had had a chance to interview Josh. Meanwhile, he had given Root a bare outline of what had been established, when Izzy had shovelled him up the chain of command. And he was immediately informed that he, Root, could well know more than the CID.

'It won't come as a surprise to you to

learn that he was one of your members, Constable Root. Name of Hancock. Mean anything to you?'

'No, sir.' Root was certain of it. 'Not come across the name during my time at Wolvers Golf Club. What's the story on him, sir?'

He was Roger Llewellyn Hancock. He had joined Wolvers twenty-nine years ago to be exact. He was then forty-one years of age, by profession a water engineer.

'Not much of a line on him so far, but your Secretary looked up the records. He'd no wallet, no watch, nothing like a rail pass, so someone's stripped the body before putting it in the ground. The metal-detector must have been over-looked, though, if concealment of the identity was in a possible perpetrator's mind. It was easy enough to trace, that, and various other indications.'

So, Gary had been right. No need to mention him.

'A fairly definite identification, though, sir, would you say? You'd find corrobora-tion of use — from Mr. Jowett, then?'

'How well,' Tomlinson had asked, 'do you, Constable Root, know this Mr. Chips?'

'Pretty well. As much as he lets you, sir.'

Root thought of the pale high forehead with the liver spots and the pince-nez dangling on the not-too-clean old paisley-patterned waistcoat. Josh Jowett lived alone. He firmly held that a Fray Bentos steak and kidney pie, the puff pastry up two inches about the lid-level together with another can, mushy peas, was a gourmet feast. With Nescafé to follow. A bit of reading a flip through the channels for an ongoing dig or an old American sitcom, then it was ten hours of deep, unconcerned sleep.

'I've not spoken to him direct, Inspector. All I have is his message. But he knows his stuff, does Mr. Jowett. Publishes articles in learned journals,' Root explained quickly. 'He's a bit of a hermit, sir. Reclusive.'

'All right. I'll get back to you, Root.'

★ ★ ★

95

And so, Root thought, we'll take ourselves off and see who looks likely for the sewing machine first. And a plod round the hub of Gritmarsh's economic life after that. Then it's off to the strawberry fields to have a chat with the local big-time agency's gangmaster about Poles who complained about their truly insanitary living conditions, and especially those who got into disputes with the local yobboes over the prettier and more adventurous girls.

Not many of them, fortunately. He could comprehend their patterns of thought. Here they were, asylum seekers, victims, so they claimed; but not quite able to retaliate when the more crazed local yobboes carried openly — on *his* patch — the spring-loaded weapons with the wickedly-honed blades that meant a fatality soon. He'd confiscate any of the murdering tools he found on the flat fields across the river.

Knives, now. And *skunk*.

Did any of Tom's mates dabble with cutlery? Beth's raucous gang with can-nabis? Constable Root made a note to himself. The comprehensive school his son and daughter attended would receive a visit soon from the back-up team all community police officers could call on. And would.

He was showing the uniform around the Gritmarsh shopping centre, not an imposing development. Quite a well-stocked DIY place. A baker's and confectionery shop. A bookie's gone posh and with three new bandits to gobble up the benefit monies. Then there was the minimalist supermarket that Sainsbury's refused to take over, even with the promise of a holiday from the rates. Mr. Chang could keep it in the family, thanks.

'So it's been a good week or two, Rosie?' Root said to the manageress. She was outside the automatic doors puffing lovingly on a Marlboro Lite. 'Mr. Chang's happy, is he? Not too many on holiday?'

'Been good, Arthur,' she told him. 'We do well with the Hong Kong jeans and the tops, what with this bit of sun we're getting.'

'For the kids?'

Wrong. 'Come on, Arthur! Don't be

such a banana. It's good fashion stuff like the skinny models wear in the tabloids. Who're you after, noseying around?'

'Just like listening to you, love.'

'You always could get round a girl, Arthur. Pity you're spoken for, like. Anyway, do something useful and do summat about my nicked trolleys.'

'How many's gone?'

'Too sodding many for Charlie Chang. Five or six in all, counting last couple of weeks. No, one more today. Seven. I reckon it's the kids from the base. Out past Hagthorpe Common. Those gippos from the 'uts that's falling apart.'

She meant the cluster of Nissen huts that had been allocated to the dozens of illegal immigrants who claimed asylum and vanished when the authorities came to check — the younger males anyway. Not much could be done with the women and the kids, however. There simply weren't enough staff in the three agencies involved to do more than put the occasional dent in the problem. The men — Romanians, whatever Rosie called them — were willing enough to work; but the Poles were more reliable, and anyway the swarthier asylum-seekers from further east had a bad reputation. They stole whatever they could. And they had settled at least three feuds with knives, though they never pressed charges or showed their wounds.

'So what's happening? The kids stealing the trolleys, that it. Rosie?'

She shrugged. 'Won't be the first to do it. Had a do when we first started them off. Got them nicked and they say the real gippos melted them down. Don't know if it's so, Arthur, do you?'

They usually got chucked into the Don. Aluminium got nicked, not steel-meshed shopping-trolleys. Or not? 'I'll look 'em up. Probably using the wheels for go-carts.'

'Wish they'd pack up their 'orses and caravans and go. I keep them out of the store, told my girls to see 'em off. Caught one of the women shovelling cans past the till, quick as owt, could hardly see her. One for the till, one or more for her daughter or whatever, quick into her bag or under that big long skirt then away with a nice smile — and someone's been at the chocolate counter, just the expensive foil-wrapped dark round ones. It's all go here, it is.'

Root said: 'Heard you still get the older ones riding their bikes in the mall.'

It wasn't much of a mall, more of a blocked off bit of road, part-covered, but with a wide pedestrian thoroughfare running its length. Which was ideal for skateboarding and cycling; the trouble was not the kids after school, though. Out of work teenagers chose to ride their mountain-bikes at speed on the pavement. And show off their skateboard skills. The women cursed them and swore they'd set their own older kids on them, but in Gritmarsh it wasn't likely to happen. The prevailing response was, more or less, well what else can the kids do? Some of them were ASBOS-labelled, and no one wanted a retributive brick through their windows, hurled by a drunken relative — of either sex — in a fit of misplaced loyalty.

Rosie said, 'Don't bother about those

two kids. They're harmless. One's suspended from the comp.'

The kids halted when they saw him.

'They ever nick anything from that posh golf club of yours?'

'Not,' he said, remembering 'Itler, 'so far as I know.'

Root's thoughts drifted.

He and Ursula had talked about Gary Brand only the night before, when Inspector Tomlinson had been on Yorkshire telly; but not him, not the lad, rather his self-proclaimed hardman father. The lad's frame had filled out. A tall, rangy youth had become a large, muscular young man. Maybe the father felt challenged. He decided to look in on Grace Warburton, now Grace Brand again, and resolutely Ursula's best friend, some time during the week. Once he'd got the Kop find sorted, to Inspector Tomlinson's satisfaction. His easy drifting stopped.

'You! Big 'at and boots! Time you were up and about!'

Arthur Root smiled at a bent little crossing lady, ready to escort the kids across the road now it was bang on twelve.

'Ginnie, duck. You going to belt them with your lollipop stick again?'

'If the little sods don't look sharp, specially those gippos. Skinny kid in fancy blue trainers marched his gang over like a procession. Nearly fell over. Reeboks would've fitted is dad. Nicked, likely. What you got to look so 'appy about?'

'Seeing you, love.'

'Ah, get off with you! You get Florrie O'Brien's Singer back!'

Then she clattered onto the road, the kids apprehensive but safely across the road, bringing a vanload of fear-struck ducks to a halt in a dismal honking of regrets. The driver saw Root and restrained himself. That was the uniform for you, thought Root contentedly.

He went to pursue his inquiries into the loss of a sewing machine. With no success at all. And more, many more, mischances, thefts, misdemeanours and complaints of this or that exhibition of bad behaviour on someone's part, real, unlikely and sometimes totally invented.

It was a busy, busy day.

He spent two hours that afternoon patrolling the unsavoury streets of Hagthorpe. He noted that one dog, a stray, was again looking for shelter and food. 'Best move on,' he told it. 'Next time, it's the pound for you.' A tail wagged. But Root had moved on.

He reflected on bits of the conversation he'd had with the CID inspector. Tomlinson had been almost complimentary about that three-year old murder at Wolvers.

'You helped in getting a result back then,' he'd said. 'Superintendent Mabbatt agrees. Nevertheless, don't think you're being detached from community policing duties, Root. You'll be made available, as when it's necessary, obviously, but the Super's happy enough with the way it's shaping up.'

Ah well, Bobbie's dignified pace, three miles an hour. A careful appraisal of doorways, or insecure bikes and cars, unattended parcels, an unwarranted accumulation of trash outside a take-away, or even a face that didn't fit, was the way he progressed; his unforced natural air of proper concern for the citizens of Gritmarsh and its surrounding villages, left a ripple of assurance in most of those he passed.

Brown, his sergeant came through as he was thinking about lunch. Normally, he'd have whizzed the old Megane back home, but today looked to be busy. 'Arthur?'

'Constable Root, responding to Control Central, Sergeant.'

'Expect a call from CID. Inspector Tomlinson's not having much success with your golfing mate. That fry-up bloke. He'll be contacting you, so Izzy says.'

6

Others found the day both a shock and a threat.

'Hancock?' And, disbelievingly, 'Not Hancock!'

'Right from Central. You owe a hundred. 'Im. Fat cop.'

'Don't do anything. Don't say anything. Got that?'

'You trying to tell me what to do?'

★   ★   ★

At about that time, the well-read and diligent Assistant Chief Constable Gerald Dundas was enjoying a *Financial Times* piece. 'Black?'

Quite a conundrum. 'A black swan,' he said to no one. 'There's a thing.' He got the call from the Chief Constable moments afterwards.

'Wolvers again, Chief? Well, well. A confirmation? And you're happy that

Superintendent Mabbat's handling it, ah, with tact? Nevertheless, I think I should at look at the situation, sir. One-armed, did you say?'

★ ★ ★

Arthur Root proceeded, conning his list of concerns. There was one he'd not given much attention to today. Drugs. Not that there were many serious users on his two patches. There wasn't enough cash around to keep more than a few youngsters going. And, again, there wasn't much to thieve and turn into spot cash hereabouts. Tellies and the like were guarded. I-pods and the newest gadgets were rareish. Schoolkids didn't readily give up their mobiles, not at Gritmarsh Comprehensive School.

Besides, the perpetrators were easily found and dealt with by the harder kids pretty soon. But skunk — that was different, for it was cheap. It was undoubtedly the drug, not of choice, but of convenience; for there was unquestionably a plantation nearby set up by

Vietnamese gangsters. Maybe green-fingered child-labourers were tending it. But, more probably, it was a local enterprise.

And why, he asked himself for maybe the thousandth time, did they want it? He knew, of course. A bit of excitement: teens rebelliousness: iconic pop stars' spangled lives. A sense of living in stupendous times and all sensations there for the asking. Cheaply, too.

'I'll get you lot,' he promised. 'Will.'

As he passed the comp, his radiophone rang. 'P.C. Root speaking.' Izzy Strapp. Not Tomlinson. Not the Super. 'Yes, I'm on patrol, Sergeant. Outside Gritmarsh Comprehensive School on Black Elms Lane.'

Then there was a somewhat jokey remark about Roger Llewellyn which was lost mostly in a vast burst of sound from a supercharged engine.

'I didn't quite get that. Traffic noise, a big bike.' Harley-Davidson, too, Root had noted, a rarity in those parts. A stranger as well. Going much too fast, and much too noisily. Gone now, and his registration not imprinted on Root's memory. 'Better, yes, with you, you say only one arm? Got it now.'

That would naturally have made the identification of Roger Llewellyn Hancock that much easier. Possibly a treasure-hunter. But, a golfer, too?

'That arm that was poking up, Izzy. Left or right?'

'It matters?' said Sergeant Strapp, who obviously didn't know.

'Not for Hancock, no. Just curiosity. He'd be a rare bird on a course.'

'The super had a word to say about that, Arthur. You know what he's like. Learned his lines from Bernard Manning that was. 'Now, on the one hand', he keeps saying? Now, here's your instructions.'

There had, he was informed, been somewhat of a difficulty. With JJ.

He was lying low, it seemed, and not available for a chat. Willing enough to give the Law the benefit of his expertise, but not just now, since he'd taken a load of medication for one of his conditions. Mabbatt had decreed that he would keep;

ailing Josh should be humoured. 'So you, Constable Root, are elected to make time to call on your Mr. Chips today with a soulful expression on your face. When's a good time — not for you, for the informant?'

'He'd want to be helpful. I'll call at his home between seven and seven-thirty.' That would be about Salsa time, Root realised. After tea, neatly depriving Ursula of a chance to get his big feet moving more precisely to the subtle interwoven beats. 'He goes off to bed early, but he's alert for a couple of hours after his evening meal.'

'Then that'll have to do.'

★ ★ ★

Now for the strawberry field and the tall, muscular Poles with their polite welcome and their disquieting way of settling disputes. He checked on the Polish-English phrase book in the glove compartment. 'Dzien dobry'. There it was. 'Gin dobry,' he said aloud, twice.

Flat and stretching for miles, with

breaks of thin and unkempt hawthorn hedging brightened here and there by a few clusters of pink and white dog roses, the fields were dotted with groups of men and some women, backs bent and wicker hampers ready. They needed the work, and it was here, and they packed away their money, most of them, to buy a four-or-five-acre farm way out in the sticks back home. Nowadays, the farms were slowly going up in price, but you could still get a hundred-year-old farmhouse with its modicum of acreage for a year's hard graft right here in South Yorkshire.

The young men he wanted wouldn't have been sending their meagre wages home. They were tall and very fit, and they had a sense of decorum when it came to chatting up the local girls. It didn't stop a run of schoolgirl pregnancies, though the Polish priest gave them merry Hell on Sundays for their sheer foolhardiness. Father Tadeusz didn't hold with good Polish lads — or bad ones, for that matter — contracting misalliances with eager apprentice tarts in short skirts and black stockings. Root voiced a thought that the priest might have come along for this chat with his strays.

'No, said he had a marriage today, and said to say sorry, Mr. Root,' the foreman-ganger told him. 'He sent Mr. Guzzbuzz along though, said you'd need someone with a good grasp of English, and he's all of that. Josef! You'll be all right with him. Bloody knives! Bad as Brixton, it's getting. Come on, police is waiting!'

Mr. Grzebieniowski said at once that his name was unpronounceable, call him Josef, and as he didn't have a mobile, never liked them, here was a card for the constable to take with him, should his services as an interpreter be needed in the courts. 'You get me at the Trades and Labour Club, Officer. I drink beer there nearly every night. I learned English in a good school, in Brighton, before the outbreak of the Second World War. I charge the usual fees for official translations, but today I am here without a penny to pay. My good friend the reverend father asks it. That O.K?'

'Well, yes. And Dzien Dobry, Mr.

— will Josef do?'

'Admirably. Shall I get the young men to come over?'

'How's their English?'

'Minimal. They're all from what you call the back of beyond. They came over about four, five, weeks ago when the picking season was just starting. 'Two can speak good German. One is out from near the Russian border, hardly knows Polish. Where do we start, Officer Root?'

They were brought to him, sheepish and sweating, one startlingly blond-haired, with pink streaks through the heavy mop.

They waited for Josef to tell them what to do, most respectful and conciliatory young men.

'What do they have to say about this feuding? Has anyone received a wound, a knife wound, that's where we start. If so, I'll have to see them individually, since we won't have that sort of thing here in South Yorkshire. This fight with the local tearaways last week. Was it over a girl?'

'Soccer,' Josef said simply. He reeked of vodka. It hadn't impacted on Root's senses at first, but it hung around the old man in a sharp cloud. 'No girls. Bad night for the lads. Their football team lost. Badly.'

'Knives? If they're around, I want them.'

'The stewards took them and stopped it before they fought,' said Josef. 'Two from our boys. It was a good crowd at Bramhall Lane, but they were careful at the turnstile.'

'The stewards caught on to it?'

'I did what was necessary under the circumstances, Officer Root.'

'Shopped them, you mean, Josef. You for United?'

The grin was sly. 'Luvvly, luvvly Rovram.'

'Rovram — oh, Rotherham!' There was a repeat, chorused and more grins. 'Can you keep them in line, Josef?'

'Course! It would be very different with the other ethnic group, the Romanians in the huts over there. They feud for a lifetime, many generations. Always blood for blood. But my lads will toe, toe — line, yes? And maybe you will pass my card on to your superior?'

Coincidence, thought Arthur Root. A

loose end that he could tweak.

'I'm thinking about it. All depends, you see. I'll put in a word with my superiors provided you can help with another matter. That's the way it works. Information, Josef.'

Gippos? The Singer? Missing steel trolleys from Mr. Chang's store?

The Poles were told to get back to picking, and Root explained what he wanted. Chiefly, it was news of marauding raids by swarthy young kids who were led, apparently, by a skinny little one who had over-large yet highly expensive Reeboks. Would Josef help?

He grinned and winked. 'That is my transportation,' he said, pointing to a mountain-bike. 'I get around for your boss right now. Would you believe I drove a T34 in the last days of World War Two?'

The radiophone burbled into life as Josef cycled away.

Inspector Tomlinson asked what he was doing. Root told the harassed-sounding CID officer that he had been following up on an incident reported to him by the local Catholic priest. One or two unrelated matters had cropped up, to do with thefts in Gritmarsh, but he was abruptly cut off.

'Constable Root, cancel that visit to your friend Mr. Jowett. He had informed me that it would be more appropriate if you met at a more suitable location. And do not laugh. And in answer to your enquiry, the deceased had lost his left arm. And Mr. Jowett wants to know if it's fine by you.'

Root couldn't help chortling silently into the mouthpiece.

'Mr. Jowett specified nine holes, then, am I right, sir? Teeing off at — I mean, starting at, was it nine? Well, certainly I can make the necessary alterations to my own schedule — '

It was turning out to be a very good day indeed.

It got better, for a madly grinning Pole with wildly-streaked hair appeared as he reached the Megane. The tall lad bowed and presented Arthur Roof with a woven basket. 'Is for missus, sir. Knives no good, O.K?'

'That's the way it is.'

7

It was not an auspicious start and Josh Jowett was not one to make light of the adverse conditions. 'It augurs not well, young Arthur.'

'The green's perfect. Bit of rain can't spoil it, can it? Besides it'll be clearing soon,' Arthur Root assured him, chancing a fabrication. 'P'raps.'

The light rain that spattered down had an unpleasant penetrative power. Cold trickles permeated the upturned collar of Arthur Root's less than Tiger-smart waterproof jacket.

The first at Wolvers was one of the great landscape features of South Yorkshire, rightly displayed on calendars and commemorated in oils as far away as somewhere called the Bright Vista Gallery in Santa Monica, California. A rich Japanese tycoon had commissioned the painting after putting down a single putt for a birdie only a year ago.

'He was always a cheat,' Josh said, when they'd driven. 'Goodish hit, by the way, Arthur. We'll find mine in a bit. About three yards into the semi — three yards?'

'Eight, ten. We'll find it.' And, Constable Root, we have about an hour and a half hour's hacking, seeking and getting wet to go, so give the informant a chance to tell it the way he wants it to come out. Bit by bit. 'Here, Josh.'

'Arthur, I can't just get it off my chest, just like that. I'll tell you this though. He were no good.'

'You'd know, Josh.'

'He'd ask you to look at the clouds or say what's that, a lark, or something like, and it might be a crow or a wing of swallows, but you wouldn't be looking.'

What was this to do with a clutch of finger bones, white at the Kop?

''Someone's left the rake down in the sand. Bad form,' he'd say. We all knew what he was doing. By the time we'd looked round and pretended to be taken in, he'd have nudged the ball on to a decent lie. You don't cheat at golf,

Arthur. Man's game. He was not straight, Roger Hancock, but I don't want to go steaming ahead with it all right away, no.'

'Take your time. What have you got for your second?'

'Five-wood. Handy tool. I like the light head and the loft. I can dig it out and get some length, if I go steady.'

He did and finished in the towering left-hand bunker, where an embedded lie had ruined many a round before it was properly under way. 'D'you think it's set in for the morning, Arthur?'

Root scanned the grey, low cloud. There was one chink in the gunmetal sky. It was not positively sunshine, rather a windowpane lit from the far side of a room by a weak tallow candle. But it was there. 'Could be.'

'Thought you'd be talkative. Your shot.'

It was a peach. The lofted club sent the ball soaring away until it dropped, held, rolled forward and finished at twelve, ten feet, Root corrected, from the hole, the insistent streamlets at his neck forgotten. A birdie chance. What a happy morning this was turning out to be, just as he'd told himself when Inspector Tomlinson had somewhat enviously told him he was to conduct an interview on the fairest vista that South Yorkshire could offer. 'Bad luck Josh,' he said to his playing companion.

JJ had already had two attempts to dislodge his ball from the sand. 'He'd have chucked it out by hand,' was the reply. 'Got it!'

The ball advanced up the sharp slope to the edge of the green, thought about rolling back, and remained, held by a worm cast on the brink of the savage sandpit. 'Two putts, and I've saved my par, Arthur!'

JJ, on the longest handicap known to golfing man, didn't subscribe to the usual way of allocating a hole the number of strokes that an expert golfer would take. His par was seven for a four-par, which was the way the first was legitimately played. Josh had his own system. No doubt his regular four-ball each had their idiosyncratic way of defining their skills. 'There, told you,' Root was informed, as

Josh putted out. 'Despite the unfavourable auguries, a good start.'

Root had missed his first putt by a whisker. The next trundled in for a more regular par than Josh's. He thought about a small screen with a needle flickering red on fluorescent green. What *had* Hancock sought at the Kop?

'Don't take to this one,' said Josh Jowett. 'Too long for me. I'll say this for Hancock, though. He'd only one wing, but he could crack a decent iron up the slope here. Straight as a die. Then he'd cheat. Couldn't help himself. Always looking for the rainbow's end.'

With an eight-inch cone projected by an Arado 120B?

The second was a much more difficult par four. What was to be Josh's next revelation?

'Did I tell you he was a Borough Waterworks technician when we had a borough waterworks?'

They'd somehow struggled to the second green. It had taken them quite a while to locate Mr. Chips' second. Root's dismal chip and run to the green had been too forceful, and his return to the hole over-hit. A six, two over par. Poor. JJ was aglow, however, since he was also down in six. By his lights, he was one under at this stage of the round. Root contemplated the maths of his system. He gave up at once. 'Wish they'd fill the pond in,' he observed, as they moved on to the long third, five hundred and twenty-eight yards from the Medal tee, twelve yards less than that for today's round. The big pond's surface almost hissed under the downpour.

'Attracts golf balls. Looks for them.'

'Reverse divination?' chuckled Josh. 'Hancock said that. He was a very skilled water engineer, did you know that, Arthur?'

'A senior technician, so CID told me, yes.'

The inspector had made sure that Izzy Strapp got in touch with the latest findings, so he knew pretty well as much as the investigating team.

Well, so, we're getting on with it, Root told himself. Slow and steady.

'He was good. Lots of better-qualified

men just didn't have his flair for watercourses. He could track subterranean channels with a couple of hazel switches, a genuine talent. Flood control was practically a mania with him. He couldn't get used to the fact that the Borough just wouldn't spend money on proper barriers, if they could avoid it. I'll tell you another thing. He was as mean as muck. Nobody got a penny from him. He'd not pike when it was his round. Didn't seem to take much pleasure in it, though. Hurried off to drink on his own, I expect. Or go somewhere cheaper. And he lived that way, too. Mean.'

'I gather he wasn't married?'

'Didn't suit him, to have a woman around, Arthur. Not reclusive exactly, just didn't let anyone know what he was like underneath.'

That got things moving on. 'You have the honour, Josh.'

'But you got a six, too. And according to my reading of the rules of golf you keep the honour by virtue of winning the first.'

'Your par-six on the last beats mine.

Forgotten you get a stroke?' Root didn't want a discussion about the rules of matchplay. He was accumulating fodder for his report quite satisfactorily. 'Taking a wood, Josh?'

'My five again. Nice little popper, Arthur.'

And for once, he hit the ball sweetly, as much as a hundred and sixty or seventy yards, straight down the fairway. So did Root. It was almost a pity to take advantage of the following wind, and the light rain — was it lessening — and set the Titleist a bit higher than usual on the peg and give it all he had.

'You do not want that one back, I tell, you, Constable Root, my lad!'

Now that Josh was into his stride, no, now that his swing was working and consequently in a far better mood than when the round had begun, Root deemed it time to delve deeper into the character of Roger Llewellyn Hancock.

'Clever, but you say he wasn't just selfish — what, untrustworthy? Pity about that, in a friend, no?'

'He was no friend of mine! Not when I

123

found he was a night-hawk!'

It was emerging. A night-hawk had to be a hunter, a thief in the dark.

'So he had this devious streak?' Root persisted, hoping to ride the obvious anger and increasing discomfort. 'Took short cuts, say?' But the moment passed, for Josh had to wheeze and hack, then give himself a couple of aerosol shots of Trinitrate.

'Heart, Arthur. Give me a couple of minutes. Makes you dizzy, but I'll be right soon. Crack a few good ones, you'll see.'

When he was breathing normally, Root chanced his luck and repeated his query about the dead man's character.

'A schemer and an opportunist, was Roger Hancock.'

And that was all. Root knew nothing more would be said about the subject for quite a while. Josh Jowett could be stubborn to the point of obduracy.

'Do I take the flag out?' he asked, at the third green.

'Just mark it, Arthur.'

So Root held the flag with the pole above the hole and waited as Josh puffed and wheezed for a few seconds, before holing a twenty-odd foot putt that didn't, as he gloated, touch the sides; though he'd hit it firmly enough to be left with a return putt of the same length if he'd been awry with his stroke.

The rain decided to leave Wolvers for the morning. With some not-too-bad golf and a lot of luck, JJ's game improved. Root played well, then badly, then very well indeed, and at the slow pull up the eighth, he knew most of what his companion was able to divulge about the life and times of Roger Llewellyn Hancock. Or, he cautioned himself, not. There was always more.

Detection had its own dark thrill, Root realised yet again.

'Gets my back,' had puffed Josh, as they followed quite decent tee-shots, him short and in the semi, Root, into what was left of the wind, his usual two-hundred-odd yards up the middle of what was known to all at Wolvers as Cardiac Hill.

'You could hire a buggy from Mick Summers.'

'Can manage. Just.'

'Buy one. Treat yourself.'

'No other bugger would!'

They were good friends, and it showed in the mild indecencies.

They walked in from the short ninth, which had been something of a triumph for both men, for they had each scrambled a par-three.

'Have you put my ramblings together yet, Arthur?' Josh had quizzed, at another stop to allow his tired old heart to recover. 'Worked out what's at rainbow's end? I can see by that predatory look on your long face you have. Well, lad?'

'Traditionally, Josh, a pot of gold. But this wasn't fairy gold, was it?'

'No, Arthur. My guess is Constantius XYZ.'

They watched a brisk young pair of golfers practising their putting.

They'd be waiting for their opponents, likely, thought Root. He waved to Mick Summers, who stood in the doorway of his shop. 'Mick.'

'Arthur. Mr. Jowett. Good half, then?'

'In and out,' said Josh. 'Expect it

though. Arthur had a steady nine.'

'The weather turned out kind.'

He would be full of curiosity, knowing quite well that Mr. Chips would have divulged a good deal of information during the long haul round the first nine. 'Mr. Church told me to look out for you, Arthur. Said he'd like a word when you got in. They're nearly done at the Kop.'

Root had seen the drab tent and the blue and white tapes the force used these days to demarcate a crime scene: 'POLICE LINE DO NOT CROSS'. A couple of white-clad figures were still taking samples. The crime — he supposed it had to be one such — was getting the full treatment. Summers waited, his eyes alive.

'Got a good line in the new Pringle sweaters. Arthur,' he said. 'Two samples I can let go at cost. Snazzy. Your size, one of them. Birthday coming? Half price, to Ursula?'

He knew better than to try to interest Josh, of course, Root grinned wryly to indicate no sale, certainly not today and highly unlikely on July the twelfth, his fortieth. 'Give me a minute, Josh, please? I'd like to put the CID officers in the picture.'

He felt a slight pressure of his shoulder. 'Sit down a minute,' Josh told him. 'Your boss will keep. You see, Arthur, I didn't tell you everything.'

'There's always little things, Josh: Some things don't always surface all at once.'

JJ considered Root's response. He found it was satisfactory.

'He was off eleven when he went missing. And he could have been down to single figures, but he was a twister there too. Didn't want a lower handicap, you, see. More cheating. And more, as I've elucidated. More fool me, not to have reported it sooner!'

'I'm listening.' Without quite under-standing the drift, though.

'Well, I did for him, didn't I? You see we weren't exactly friends, but we had the same obsessive common interests.'

'And you did — what?'

'I reported him. I got him black-balled.'

Guilty conscience. That was it. Well, Josh Jowett wouldn't be the first outraged golfer to put in a quiet word with the Secretary, or even the President of the Management Committee about some long-term form of reprehensible behaviour on the part of a fellow-member.

'So you took appropriate steps, Josh. You did right. Who did you speak to?'

'Speak? I wrote, of course!'

'And that did the trick? Got him barred?'

'At once!'

'So no more golf for Hancock, then?'

'Golf, Arthur? Golf! This isn't about anything so trivial, man! Are you out of your mind? Don't you have an inkling of how serious his misconduct was? He was a disgrace to our calling!'

'Which was, Josh?'

'Why the pursuit of knowledge, of course! The one indisputable way of verifying the Past!'

The pot of fairy gold that wasn't from Fairyland. Was it ever, though? 'Well, what have you to tell me, sir?'

'The man was nothing more than a common looter!'

8

When he spotted Phil Church striding over to where Root still sat, Josh Jowett was on his feet, creakily, but with determination. 'Enough! I've said all I wish about this miserable situation. Any more I might say will undoubtedly make matters worse. Here.'

He held out a five-pound note.

'Get off with you, Josh.'

'Very soon, almost immediately. But fair's fair, despite my particular interpretation of the card. Spend it frivolously and farewell. I don't want to know anything about that misnamed Anglers Kop ever again! You won't let them pester me, will you?'

Root could evade the truth with ease. Gold, death, a hidden mystery. It could hardly rest. 'I'll fend them off,' he said. 'For now.'

'Knew I could trust you, Arthur.'

'Right you are, Josh,' he said. 'You need

a bit of calm. Do the crossword — *Guardian*, isn't it? Have a couple of nips, too. It's gone one o'clock. And get yourself some food, will you do that for me?'

Jowett nodded furiously, looked pitifully at the large bay windows of the members' bar and fled to his Fiat Uno.

Arthur Root watched him go, a strange and lonely figure. He told Phil Church that he would meet him in the bar in a half-hour. 'Official, you see, Phil.'

He showered, then he was ready to phone in his preliminary findings.

It was a story that took Sergeant Strapp's fancy, once he had absorbed the facts, which took valuable time. District CID was overstretched.

'Out on a slash, then a burn,' Izzy said, about Inspector Tomlinson a CDI and Superintendent Mabbatt. 'Three Paki kids, oldest no more than five. Two confirmed dead. Attercliffe way. Could be what they call an honour job, these days. Pretty mum shaking her sari at the wrong bloke, they think. And they won't be back, not during your shift. The burn's nasty, too. No kids, thank god. Me, I've got five minutes. And did you say a pot of gold? Is this Enid bleeding Blyton-land or what, Arthur?'

The pot of gold, Arthur Root was forced to explain, was hypothetical so far as concrete and stand-up evidence was concerned. His trusted friend and fellow-golfer had sworn that Hancock had stolen a third-century hoard of Romano-British gold coins, probably in excess of four hundred, about what the sleek earthenware pot would contain. And had spirited them away over twelve years ago, at which time he himself, that is, Hancock, had disappeared, believed to have taken himself off to Spanish Morocco, there to investigate reports of recent similarly lucrative finds.

'Forget where he's gone. And when. Just the gold. This pot was nicked?'

'That is what Mr. Jowett tells me.'

'Full of Roman coins nicked by Hancock, right, Arthur. This is this Mr. Chips' story? A jam-jar full?'

'Correct, but a pot. Like an amphora. And unopened at that time, since the finder died on the day that he located the Constantantius hoard. It was stoppered, by two coins of a low denomination, I'm told. And, yes, stolen.'

Izzy Strapp was deft with the gadgetry. He had checked whilst chatting. And his searches had confirmed what Root already knew. 'Nothing.' Yet he was intrigued, and more minutes ticked by. 'Run it by me again, will you, Arthur? It's knocking my little grey cells around, I can tell you.'

Here was more than a mystery. For Josh had told Boot that when an elderly gentleman-archaeologist called Tobias Simmonds had made the one and only significant find of his treasure-seeking life then he, that fervid hunter, had died shortly after making, literally, the find of a lifetime.

'So how did your mate get hold of this, Arthur?'

'Circuitously. We haven't got that far today. Mr. Jowett, that's my golfing friend Josh, hasn't yet told me all. Most of it, but he's holding back. I don't believe he's implicated in anything illegal. I'm not sure why, but I know he's being cagey. You know, this really is a CID matter, Izzy.'

'It isn't on the data base. We go back more than twenty years now. No crime reported concerning a Romano-British hoard of the second Constantine period. Nor the first, mate. Not even done him for parking his chariot. And no reference to a Mr. Tobias Simmonds. Or a Joshua Jowett, for that matter.'

No crime reported, no investigation, so no record. It was a blank.

'Told you, Izzy, no one believed Josh when he tried to shop Hancock. I got that far, but not all of it. He's holding something back.'

Izzy Strapp was loving it. 'You keep at it, Arthur. Don't worry, the super's going to be interested. He's been asking what we thought this Hancock did next in the Hokey-Cokey. He'll be there. When he's done with a few other matters, murder and so on, machetes and cans of petrol, that sort of thing, maybe not today though. You off for some more golf, then?'

Arthur Root had his lunch with the Secretary instead of Josh.

The bar-lounge was fairly busy, so they sat at a table at the back of the enormous and ornate former drawing room by a latticed window that overlooked not much more than a dense grove of rhododendrons, whilst Josie Marsden took their order.

'So it's all going to come out, Arthur. Usual, my dear. That right? A beer?'

'Tea for me. What's the reaction so far, Phil? I didn't know Hancock, well before my time, but quite a few of the older members must have known him. And you know I can't repeat anything that Josh Jowett might have said to me, we'll take that as definite?'

'Nothing much goes unnoticed here, Arthur. We all knew that the man wasn't really our sort. When you go into the rough and find you've got a bad lie then it's between your conscience and yourself not to make it better Josh Jowett wasn't the only one to see what he was up to. He was asked to leave, you know, I can go that far.'

It had been made known to Roger Lewellyn Hancock that he could cease to be a member by resigning discreetly. Twelve or thirteen years ago, it was suggested to him that he might fail to renew his subscription; just sort of forget to send the cheque or cancel the standing order, then he'd be quietly taken off the list. No one on the Committee wanted him carpeted and kicked out. Never happened in a hundred years.

'Tactful, Phil.'

They talked for a while, Phil mostly about Hancock; whilst Arthur Root was at pains to explain that he himself would have little to do with the ongoing investigation into the mystery of his death.

Phil's flabby face tautened.

'The treasure-hunting, Arthur. We knew about that, of course. Freddie's halfblind now, but he had sharp eyes back then. He knew that Hancock was quartering the fields with his metal-detector. Did it systematically, on a grid pattern. Freddie would know. He was Army during the National Service days.'

'This would be on the Kop?'

'Richardson land then, so nothing to do with us.'

Hancock was just another form of scavenger, so far as Freddie was concerned. Kids looking for treasure came across bit of the detritus of battle all the way down the Don. 'He hadn't much time for chancers, our Freddie.'

'I'll pass it on, Phil.'

'Expected no less. So, we just await developments, Alice and the Major and the rest of us I expect? I thought your inspector handled it well on the box, by the way. With aplomb. Alice and her Ted were impressed. What will you do with the rest of your day?'

'Not golf. It's back into uniform for me. Oh, I'm paying if I can get a chit from Bliss. This can come off CID expenses, Phil. We'll have a knock soon, yes?'

He wasn't finished with Wolvers yet, though, for Major Wynne-Fitzpatrick hailed him as he was about to fire up the

Megane. 'You, man!'

The roar of command held Arthur Root frozen, till his wits returned and he saw it was the Captain. 'Sir!'

'Want you to know. Didn't know the man, before my time here, but this Hancock was a scoundrel and deserved all he got,' was the Major's opinion. 'Wouldn't take a drink here, went off to some low-life public house to do his boozing. And what's this about him making off with some sort of loot? Seen enough of it in my time, but you wouldn't think a member here would be involved. What the devil are you doing about it?'

'You know how it goes, Major. Rules. Precedents. The Law.'

Farseeing and still far away eyes fixed on him.

'Rules? Ah, Quite! See now. Right way to do it. Yes. Another thing, Arthur, blessed greenkeeper's wanting to know what about these damned gippos; especially a cheeky one with a leather chain round his neck, little devil. What do you know, then, Arthur?'

'What I don't, I'll find out, Alf. You in

for the Pro-am-am-am next week, then?'
'They are not keeping me out of it!'

* * *

Arthur Root was back into the uniform. Now, there were the regular duties to take care of, the most important of which was to show a police presence.

I will plod, he determined, as a plod should. But sleuth around too.

His radiophone buzzed as the thought came into his head.

'Constable Root speaking. This is a police officer. Please speak now.'

'Get round to our Grace's, Arthur. For pity's sake. Now, love!'

9

He would not be resuming his usual duties, so he told Control. Bill Brown phlegmatically acknowledged his news.

'What is it, just a domestic?'

'It looks that way, Sergeant.'

My domestic, he found himself wanting to say.

'Be Gary,' he found himself saying aloud and hoping fervently it was containable, as he reached Gritmarsh's thoroughfare. Gary wouldn't stand for his Ma getting knocked about. Just then, a black-clad rider zoomed past him.

The Harley-Davidson again? No doubt of it. And still he missed the number plate, for it was, he saw now, partly concealed by what had to be a custom-made set of panniers. Were they artfully placed to deceive? Could be.

Black-clad, a biggish and youngish figure, rocketing — where?

It would come. Right now, he was

turning into Orchard Close and then onto the short bricked driveway, and there was bloody, literally bloody, Danny Warburton slouched on the drive, with Gary pale and trembling at the doorway, and his mum behind him; and Ursula watching out for him, the police, her husband, and Gary's one hope of getting away from, possibly, an assault charge. Danny was trying to crawl. One leg was buckled. Please, Root begged, not a break. All we could do with, a GBH on the lad. Gary's fists were still clenched, the shakes very much evident. Ursula looked tired and wild still. It took an effort of will for him to keep from reaching for her.

'Arthur! He hit her again!'

'G-bb-getthat — sod!' Warburton was growling through blood and snot. And Arthur Root felt no compassion for him whatsoever.

'Called for an ambulance?' he asked, as he slid easily from the Megane. 'No? Wait.' Maybe it would not be necessary to ask for immediate assistance of an overstretched service. 'Warburton, keep still. We'll take it a step at a time. Gary, look him over — do it!'

Warburton shook his big, bloodied head. Grace regarded him with horror. Root saw that she had her hand to her left eye. She was partly covering her nose too. Root sensed his own rage building as his wife spoke:

'Arthur? What's to happen?'

'I can't overlook this matter, Ursula, you know that as well as I do. You listening, Danny? This is a police matter now. Gary?'

'No real damage. My mum's probably worse off than this bastard.'

'Grace, put your hand away, love. Is the skin broken?'

That made a difference, blood, an open wound — just as any slight fracture of any bone in the big sod's body would have made a difference, a prodigious one, for what could be held to be a common assault could easily become grounds for a charge of Grievous Bodily Harm, with its attendant heavy penalties. The women clung to one another, whilst Warburton levered himself upright. 'Gary?'

Grace was marked, but not wounded.

'Ursula, get inside with Grace,' he ordered. 'You've done well, love. Tea, sugar for both of you. And the lad.'

Danny Warburton tried to look fiercely at his son. He came out with a mouthful of abuse. Root caught the stench of stale beer with an overlay of spirits. This was Danny's tipple. He'd order a pint of beer, sip a little, and top it up with as much vodka as he could afford. Certainly he had taken quite a few. Automatically, Root checked his watch. It was only twelve minutes since he'd left Wolvers. He groaned mentally. Another unnecessary complication in their lives. Warburton was searching the gravel.

Gary explained. 'His dentures came out, Arthur.'

One hand searched for the yellow teeth. And there they were, the top set anyway. More abuse followed.

'If these are badly broken,' he began.

'Oh, leave it, will you, Danny?'

Gary was still breathing hard. His cold stare at his father told of his still fiery rage. 'Easy, Gary. Give me a minute, then you can tell me what happened, all right?'

Warburton was trying to fit the upper set into his mouth as Root considered his options. He had none. The man was a violent and malicious sot. 'Sergeant Brown, please,' he said into his radio-phone. 'Root. Arthur Root. I'm at thirteen Orchard Close, Gritmarsh. The householder is Grace Brand. There's been a serious domestic dispute. I wish to detain a suspect. Yes, Warburton, Daniel. The man is quiet at present, but intoxicated. Yes. Alcohol. Heavily.' Bill Brown had only a couple of questions. 'Yes.' Root agreed. 'Well known.'

That was the way of things. Meanwhile, he asked a few questions and found that it was the usual thing. Gary's disowned father had come yet again on the pretext that he wanted his marriage back. And when his approaches didn't work, it hadn't taken him long to start bellowing and bulling his way into the house. Probably he wasn't aware that his son was around.

'You just hit him once, Gary?'

'It was enough. In the gut. He was going for mum. He puked right away. I was making scrambled eggs for us. She tumbled down the stairs, that's when she blacked out. Auntie Ursula came round right away. I chucked him out onto the drive before she got here. Then you came. Knew you would. You always do.'

'That's enough for now, lad. Here's the squad car.'

'So what happens?'

'Depends, that's all I can tell you.' Domestics were never easy. The harm and the hurt remained, but often a victim wanted no more of it and wouldn't make a formal accusation. 'They'll put him in the cells for a few hours, then decide.'

'What about me?'

'As it stands, you've assaulted your father. But I can't see it going badly for you. He entered without permission. Grace is hurt. He could be charged but that depends on the Duty Inspector.'

Root considered that Warburton might well get away with a caution. He thought of the terror on Ursula's friend's white face.

'Danny,' he said quietly. Bleary eyes regarded him with hate, threatening violence. His own banked-down fires momentarily flared. 'Just a word from me to you.'

Gary watched and waited. He knew that this tall, lean, well-mannered police officer who was now his friend had faced down the worst that Hagthorpe and Gritmarsh's serious brawlers could try on him. And here was his own father, sensing the power in this quiet man. He could see the defiance fade and the clenched fists open, the fingers now palsied. Danny Warburton was unable to withstand the promised retribution he saw in that implacable stare. 'Don't come here again,' he heard Arthur Root say in an almost whispered, feral undertone that only he and his father, could make out. Do you understand? Never!'

Danny Warburton didn't stay to hear any more. He levered himself up and lurched towards the squad car. Brown had come personally, for which Arthur Root was grateful. A hulking and very young constable was out of the car in a moment, well before the sergeant. Big and menacing though he looked, Warburton advanced more or less steadily towards the safety of the Law. His chin was down on his big, heavy chest, almost to the slope of his round beer-belly. No, Gary told himself. Danny wouldn't be back.

'He won't be back, Arthur,' he said.

He was to remember his words. And soon.

'You see to things here, Constable Root,' Sergeant Brown said. 'Drop by about five, will you? Come on, sir,' he said to Warburton. 'In the back with this officer.'

'You always come when you're needed, don't you, Arthur?'

She was back at the door, her face flushed, but her eyes alive.

Arthur Root could find nothing to say to his wife. It seemed a long time since the peace of the day's golf had been shattered by the whooping cry for help from the JCB. What, he wondered, between mayhem and fire, was the super making of it all? Not, he told himself, my problem.

There was the rest of the day to get through.

★ ★ ★

Superintendent Mabbatt was unaware of Root's difficulties. At present, he was fending off the Assistant Chief Constable's wish for news of progress at that toffee-nosed golf club; and clearly he was himself being pressured too. They were in fairly comfortable padded chairs in an airy office overlooking a canal basin that was in the process of becoming a marina.

'It gets intriguing, Joe,' the ACC agreed. 'This Root's a canny one. Getting in at the side door with the amateur archaeologist. Did he win?'

Mabbatt took a moment. Golf? Bloody hell!

He let it pass, once he saw that this was an example of Dundas's sly humour. 'In fact, I've detailed a good team to investigate something quite promising that could get us looking at a result.'

'And that is?'

'Well, you know that the late Mr.

148

Hancock put his goods into storage when he went to Spanish Morocco.'

'He'd stash his loot in a depository? Is that credible?'

'That will come out, I expect, sir. Always does, in the end.'

'And? I can see by that smirk on your big face that you're not done.'

Mabbatt wasn't. 'Constable Root's a good beat officer,' he said. 'But to get to the bottom of things needs a good brain and a talent for detecting. That's what we do best, sir. Our job.'

⋆   ⋆   ⋆

Time passed for Arthur Root.

He showed the uniform to a good part of Gritmarsh's outer and more affluent district. The dog was there again, when he returned to check the mall. The RSPCA might do something; but he'd promised the abandoned creature some time.

I'm tired, he thought, realising that the day had been too long and far too packed with harsh and deep emotions — violence and old bones

149

He got through to Ursula on a landline.

'How's Grace, love?' Ursula was silent. 'Just tell me she's all right, will you?'

'She'll never be all right so long as that — that swine's around.'

'She with you?'

'Yes, making jam, Arthur.'

'And Gary?'

'I don't know where he is. She's worried about him. Find out, Arthur.'

Sergeant Brown had news both good and bad. Gary had called in at the station; and his father had been released. As Root had supposed, Grace wouldn't press charges.

'He cooled off?'

'Soberish. The duty inspector wanted the cell free.'

'And he's gone where, Bill?'

'Who cares? Do you?'

Have to, thought Root. I have to. 'And Gary? How did he seem?'

'You on your way home, Arthur? No big problem, but it's best we have a quiet word here. Just bob in for a few minutes, will you? It's nothing much but it wants clearing up.'

An informal summons like that would not have anything to do with the Hancock investigation. CID would be involved. So, Gary.

They had arranged to meet in the canteen.

'Your lad, Arthur,' said Brown in the busy pastel-walled canteen, mug of tea in his red fist. 'You know he came in to see me?'

'Not till you told me. That would be not so long ago?'

'Fourish. He was in a flap, since he's got the offer of a few days' driving, so he didn't want to stay long. Just long enough to give me his side of things when that no-use father of his went berserk.'

Gary would take any work he could get.

'It's sorted then, Bill? You said no charges, Grace wouldn't shop him. I can't say I blame her. But he could do with being collared. And the lad, Bill? He won't be charged?'

'No.' Brown showed his discomfiture. 'You won't like this. Got to be said though.' He paused, and seeing that Root wasn't becoming alarmed, which didn't surprise him, he went on, 'Didn't come out when I first had a chat with him. But he was bothered. See, it was the fact that his father had gone upstairs, and then Grace followed him. That got Gary's rag — I don't have to join the dots, I know, Arthur.'

Yes. There had been a mention of the stairs. Some memories were best left undisturbed. 'No.' There would be a sense of utter outrage in Gary's thinking, if he was still capable of rational thinking by that time. 'It doesn't need much putting together, Bill.'

Brown looked relieved. It was a touchy matter, for over the years Warburton had been to the house several times when he was steaming drunk to the point where he entertained a fantasy of still being a husband. With conjugal rights.

'Touchy. Thing was, Arthur, it was Danny that went upstairs first — Grace only followed to try to get him to leave. That's what she told Gary afterwards. She wanted him out before her lad could intervene. She was trying to protect him from Danny, but it didn't work out.'

'He'd be a fool to think our Grace would have anything to do with him. Which leaves why, right — why? That it? Why go upstairs?' he said, trying to visualise the course of events. 'And to which bedroom? That's if he wasn't trying for the bathroom and the lavatory?'

Gary hadn't got that far, so he'd told Bill Brown. He'd been embarrassed and furious in the telling of it, in an almost incoherent outburst, till he got hold of himself and calmed down. But it wasn't the toilet facilities.

'Leaves one thing, right, Arthur?'

It didn't take much working out for a police officer of Root's experience. It was obvious that Danny Warburton had all but broken into Grace's house with an express purpose. 'After something.'

Brown nodded. 'You find out, do that?'

'I'll get onto it right away. When Grace is more settled.'

'Not been much of a day for you, after all?'

'Could have been worse. Yesterday was productive, though.'

Root told him about the gimlet-eyed ancient Pole who went to war in armour five inches thick, and a Romany kid who would bear investigation. 'I'll write it up at home,' he finished. 'Oh, forget the knives issue. The new lads in the fields know the score now. So, how about Wolvers, Bill?'

They talked about gold and bones, or Bill Brown did.

He told his colleague and friend that nothing much had gone forward in the Hancock matter, not that he had heard anyway. CID had established that the dead man had probably rented a storage container, but there was no confirmation yet. Nor that he had died by another's hand. The post-mortem wasn't yet under way. Hancock's death might or might not give rise to a full murder investigation; for the moment, the remains of the riverine archaeologist-golfer would be in a cold tray, awaiting Dr. Anderson's attention. That was all that Izzy Strapp had told him; except that he'd been assigned to the matter of Hancock's material possessions, possibly still rotting away in a container, and that he'd been putting his little grey cells to work on just where; and his new DC had one or two ideas, so she did. 'Oh, and that young CID inspector's going to see your golfing mate. It seems the metal-detection fraternity got their knickers in a twist with one another. Lots of backbiting and dissension, if not what the lawyers call downright acrimony. Goes beyond jealousy, apparently. Suppose it would over a pot of gold like your mate surmises. What was it you call him?'

'That'll be our Mr. Chips, Bill.'

The time had passed quickly. Six-forty, and tea would be ready.

*　*　*

Ursula was weepfully glad to see him.

Grace had gone when he returned. She wanted to get back to work — she did agency nursing — and she felt she had to get back to a routine, it helped, looking after someone else, and anyway, she had to keep the house going, didn't she? But she didn't feel up to having a meal with them; and anyway Gary had rung through on her mobile to ask how she felt and what she was doing. He'd liked it that she was with her friend and reminded her that he was fond of strawberry jam. Meanwhile, the old white Transit van he was driving for Mr. Khan had got a flat and the spare wasn't fit to put on. And they weren't in any roadside association, so he was stuck out in the Peak District waiting for a replacement — which would have to come from a car-breakers, that being what Mr. Khan vowed was all he could afford. 'And I just don't feel like going to Harrogate on Saturday either. Oh, I don't know what I want! If that swine comes near her again — '

'The kids,' said Root gently. 'They want to eat. So do I.'

10

Contrary to Sergeant Brown's information, things were moving — albeit laterally and not fast — in the matter of Roger Llewellyn Hancock. Mrs. Godalming, for one, had made certain connections. She had a great deal of affection for her partner, and she didn't want, if at all possible, she qualified, his particular apple-cart in any way disturbed, let alone upset.

They had finished dinner and were ready for a half-hour of drama.

'No, I'll record the programme,' Alice Godalming announced. 'I need a little while to talk to you, Ted. You'll have guessed already, you always are four steps ahead of me. And most others.'

'Most unlikely, my dear. So, please tell me what troubles you.'

'I'm not exactly sure. But you know about gold, don't you?'

'Never kept it away from you, Alice. In

my business, I have to. It's been my life since Rotterdam, nineteen-forty.'

He had long since told her of his past and how he, a boy destined for the camps, via the Dutch police, had come to be spared the Holocaust. Gold had saved him, so it was not unusual for any kind of transaction to be his livelihood now. It was well known throughout the North that Ted Jones could find funds for any promising start-up business; or, equally, take in a group's guitars and drums for a week or two in one of his pawnbrokers' shops till they got the promise of a gig or two.

'I can't help thinking you'd know about Roger Hancock and this supposed pot of gold that came his way.'

'Well, you do like a mystery. And crime was your profession, in a manner of speaking, Alice.'

'These treasure-hunters. You've known some?'

'I prefer not to deal with them. Especially since the Treasure Trove legislation came in. All finds have to be reported and documented, for historical accuracy about this sceptred isle.'

'From what I've heard they're in it for the money, the hell with improving our knowledge of our island heritage.'

'Not all of them. But quite a lot get heavily turned on once they come up with their first pound coin on the beach, then their first jewelled ring. It goes on from there, then you'll get a group banding up to work on a likely site together. This area's rich in Romano-British hoards, Yorkshire, Lincolnshire — all reachable easily in an hour from here. But nowadays there's so many at it, you can't find a field that's not been scoured. Permission to search a field isn't easy to find. Farmers generally don't want twenty or so people crisscrossing over their land. Some do, of course.'

'They get greedy, Ted, yes?'

They had lived together as equal and sedately happy partners for the better part of a year now. Alice's late husband, not his first marriage, had died demented and sedated, leaving less of a fortune than Alice had been led to expect. His daughters had homed in, accompanied by legal vultures.

She had not found her new partner's wealth a burden.

'Greedy? Anyone can be, given the right opportunity.'

'Like the captain at Rotterdam?'

Ted Jones, as he was now, had been on the last boat to leave Rotterdam as the Stukas finished off the port installations and sank three cargo vessels to seal it off. The captain of the fourth took them off. The offer from the Jewish Agency was irresistibly large and in gold, too. Someone had taken a photograph of the last ship out of the port, with the children crowding the rails, mostly without an adult, some of the boys with fedoras and ringlets, or skullcaps and gaberdine coats.

'I don't think I told you it was my mother who sewed the eight gold bars into my waistcoat. But she told me not to part with them till the ship left harbour. It was the last time I saw her. She went to look for my father.'

'And you were eight, and you knew to do that.'

'It was grow up time, Alice.'

She looked at him. Not big. Hard. He would have done what he had to.

'Do you know who took Hancock's rainbow gold?'

'I have my suspicions, but we'd best leave that to the experts to find out. Can we re-run it now — I don't much care about whose baby it is, I just like the chat in the Vic. where it left off. Yes?'

Alice Godalming knew when to close a conversation. '*Eastenders* it is. To the Vic, then, Ted. And I already know who's the father.'

★ ★ ★

Gary had slept in the Transit van. His dilemma was simple. He had a load of Aziz Khan's bales of fabric aboard, as much as the one-tonner could take without the shockers giving up. He had been told that he was carrying a fortune and that he was to keep it as safe as he would his own precious mother, Gary, my son.

Safe. The decision made itself. He

found a bundle of softish velour curtaining ends and stretched out on a narrow space at the back.

Gary thought of Josie's cleavage, which kept him awake for some time. So did the memory of his father's big clunking fist aimed at his mother's slender neck. He thought sleep was impossible.

Josie, now. He had her mobile number somewhere.

* * *

Night came late. At midnight, the big, heavy-bodied man cursed as he found his boot entangled. He kicked out, spewing acid and phlegm in a foul burst of rage. The van was hidden in a riverside growth of blackthorn and dog roses, with brambles snaking out over an ill-defined path. This was a rendezvous that only necessity and fear had forced him into. He fingered the talismanic offering deep in his old donkey jacket pocket. The giveaway yellow reflector was gone from its back. He wanted secrecy and privacy, but most of all the reassurance that his business with the man he was to meet would remain private.

Old ghosts would not walk. Distant memories could be suppressed, and the easygoing life he had known for so many years would continue, with only the occasional surge of adrenaline to add a little spice in the darkest moments. A quick flurry of blows to justify a perceived insult; or a single drilling punch into a tottering youth's slack-jawed, booze-fuddled face. Good. Maybe even a real fight, just once in a while, to recall the baying of shocked and over-excited men and women who could rise from their seats, all safe, all vicariously triumphant and all well protected from harm, with the blood not theirs and anyway only spattering the canvas and the ropes and sometimes — horror and ecstasy! — speckling a dress or a shirt: the punters were not in any danger. And he could pity them. They could never know the incandescent glory of destroying a man. The sense of gut-wrenching blood-lust was his alone And just now he wanted to be what he was, had been, wanted again to be the destroyer; to feel the power of his heavy shoulders and fists driving into a face. *His*.

'Damn right,' he agreed. 'Him as well.'

He neared the edge of a gap in a stretch of corrugated-iron fencing.

Patches of rust looked black in the feeble moonlight. The rest had a faint sheen. It looked like the colour of death. He cursed again, this time aloud, for the moon was behind thin, high cloud, and the pallid iron was black. He could not make out the carefully concealed private way beyond the high, barbed wire topped fence.

He listened for a hint that his old accomplice — never mate, he told himself in angry dismay, never someone you could share a drink and a joke with — might be nearby. But all he heard was a slapping of water against a bank of rock and slime. And then chimes as a distant Norman church rang out tinnily down the gorge of the Don. He spat. The half-bottle in his pocket held a last mouthful. He let it sluice around his few blackened teeth and then slide down his thick throat. The bastard. 'You there?'

Past twelve now, Danny Warburton told himself. Late.

Then he was suddenly glad, for he could hear the rustle of legs pushing undergrowth aside. And then came the welcome sound of metal scraping on metal. 'About bloody — '

Blows fell on his thick skull. Again and again.

In his remaining nanosecond of consciousness, he knew he had lost this one. Falling, his synapses tried to make out whether it would be a better payout in consequence: he could not recall whether he should dive, or had done so already.

He was not aware of the arrangements that had been made for him. And, of course, he did not hear until some time later the whine of a starter that brought machinery alive: the intended instrument of his death.

★ ★ ★

Gary awoke after a full five hours of deep sleep. It was as much as he'd hoped for. It seemed as though only two or three minutes had drifted away when a bellowing and banging had him reaching for weapons. 'In theer! You the bloke with the flat tyre? Gritmarsh lad? Old Paki's driver, like?'

A half-hour later, Gary drove away, found a sidetrack he knew with a twenty-four hour smallish filling station. He had a couple of ten-pound notes for petrol and food. He debated whether or not to spend money on his mobile. Hunger won out.

His mother kept trying the number.

'I need to talk to you, son. Gray, pick up. Answer, lad!'

★　★　★

Danny's death came slow as dawn came up, red and pale clouds over the winding stretch of the river.

That he could wrench himself from the grip of the shrieking metal all around him said much for his sheer brute strength. That he was alive at all was something of a fluke. Two blows on the

166

head had flung his brain about his thick skull far more violently than any punches he had suffered before. Soft sand in wool left no indentation; the effects were neurologically devastating. Yet brain still functioned, if at the lower levels of consciousness. He was left with only an instinct for survival. His arms reached out and found metal all around him. *Van.* There was no coherent plan in his next moves. Simply, he heard the crusher seizing on metal. He kicked out at metal doors, then picked himself up as he had done so many times before and lumbered towards the moonlit framework of the whining jaws. He felt his right leg seized. Pain incandescently jerked the torn flesh and shattered bone free. The mass of machinery shuddered. Gears locked, and he could feel black metal closing on him. A roar of fury and his last reserves of strength had him out of the hellish trap. Then he fell into the night's blackness, unnoticed by the attendant murderer, busy with the controls of the towering crusher.

Danny Warburton instinctively crawled

away. Dark blood gushed onto shards of metal and soaked straggling weeds. He heaved and crawled and wrenched his exhausted frame away and down a slope he somewhere identified as familiar. Down again, the pain now an unavoidable torment as nerve-endings slid onto shattered bone. A shrill whimpering was all he could utter as his shoulders and head met chill, swirling water. The current took him.

★   ★   ★

Strapp and Amy Briggs didn't make it to the storage depots for another two days. No one panicked when there was a rush of work. They had to prioritise. That meant house-to-house enquiries for all available bodies in the two big investigations that were keeping Superintendent Mabbatt both busy and happily furious. Things were normal at CID headquarters. On Friday morning, he was on the road at eight with the new woman DC. They'd not had much to say to one another.

'See what you can get out of this lot,' instructed Strapp.

They'd been to one depot already, but they were at the wrong place. So much was quickly established. A smiling receptionist took two minutes to check the databases and, no, sorry; but she said she could see it was important, so they might try Massie's Storage, who weren't international and not really a big carrier at all, but who handled a lot of the local trade.

Much of police work was the same. Eliminating one source, trying another possibility. With a bit of luck, you got there eventually. Not this morning, though.

'Would he have used them, Izzy? It doesn't sound like the firm the sister heard about. Didn't she say Hancock was penny-pinching?'

Inspector Tomlinson had asked for assistance from the South Wales force. She had been co-operative to a point, but she wished to have no part in any investigation. Hasn't seen him since long before he came to South Yorkshire, doesn't want to hear about a will or a house or anything at all, for that matter. She wouldn't say anything about what he was like. 'There's some sort of history between them,' he'd said to Strapp the day after the identity had been confirmed, 'but nothing specific. She's a widow. And she knows about police matters — she was a social worker in Swansea for the whole of her working life. Sixty-seven now and all she wants is to be left alone.'

'No other relatives, sir?'

'None, according to Mrs. Anne Wilcox. And what she does know came to her by a roundabout route, some connection with a work colleague. You and DC Briggs get busy on it.'

And here they were, at a decent, if small set of premises. 'Here we go then, Massie's, Briggs. All yours.'

'Amy? Remember?'

Strapp grinned. He knew she could deal with the manager, who was predictably impressed by having a good-looking rather petite fresh-faced young woman on the premises. 'Alan Barker, that's me, Detective.'

'No worries,' said the manager, who

looked as though he coped easily with his job. Telephones whined. He ignored them. An office worker signalled to him from an inquiry window. He waved her in. 'Let's have some details, then I'll run it by our records. Phyllis, you'll have to do it the hard way. Some coffee whilst you're waiting — before we got IT,' he explained. 'Won't take long. Sergeant? Young lady? I'm thinking coffee.'

They refused. It was not much past nine-thirty. It looked as though it could be a long morning. Phyllis came back to confirm them in their thinking. Hancock had not left his goods with Massie' Storage. Again, coffee was offered, and this time accepted, for Amy Briggs had given Strapp the narrow-eyed look that meant: more.

'It's going back a fair bit,' DC Briggs suggested. 'Eleven, twelve years, Mr. Barker.' And the police would appreciate his advice.

He agreed. It was a long time. Too long. Three months was too long.

'Space is money, and we rely on rents and a quick turnaround for an empty container. When I started here, we'd got the records in a mess and we turned up one entry for a container that hadn't been serviced — that's paid for — for six years. Twelve, though!'

'Things different, I expect, sir,' said Strapp. 'Changed, say?'

'Had to change, Sergeant. We take three months in advance, under our standard agreement. But, no rent, no owner forthcoming, and — well, that's commerce. Not that we're hard and fast with the conditions. Things can go wrong with payments. Banks cock things up, granted, but people can disappear, you know. Just drop out of life, like. Is this helping?'

It was. Like all those of his profession, Strapp could wait and listen and show no especial sign of interest when a glimmer of light began to show.

'It is, sir,' Amy said. 'How many do default — say out of a hundred?'

The manager ceased to think of the young woman as a prospect. 'Three, or thereabouts. Just gone.'

'So I expect you dispose of the goods, Mr. Barker?'

'Auction them off. We do it all right and legal. Lucky, though, if we get fifty quid for a load of furniture, the way things are now. You could be in for thousands if you let things go. And don't ask me what happens to the difference between what we get and what's owed. We always lose out.'

'And if I said that the party we've got in mind isn't known for his generosity, would that help you to point us in the right direction, sir? Oh, thanks. Smells good.'

The coffee was excellent, and Barker was a perceptive man.

'Down market firms? There's a few about. I know of a couple you wouldn't want your old dad to use when he went into care, if you know what I mean. But if you say your man's as mean as muck, I'd suggest skipping them and get right to the bargain basement.'

Izzy Strapp said that he was sure D.C. Briggs meant just that.

'I've got one name in mind, but I don't know if they're still in business. They were a few years back, but they're not really competition.'

'They'll be who, sir?'

'Crakes. Quite a way from here, up the valley Sheffield way. Were, now — ? Got it. Burngreave. Phyllis will look it out for you. Brothers.'

He made a down-pointing gesture that told them enough. He went to the window, where two men and a stripling were unloading a monstrous removal trailer. 'We keep our staff. I can't say the same for them.'

'We're taking up a lot of your morning, sir.'

'Miss, you're not wasting my time, don't think it for a moment. This can be a dodgey sort of trade, what with maybe quite valuable stuff in our containers. Possibly items we wouldn't want to store if we knew, though we're careful to have the dogs sniff around, know what I mean? Anyway, we have to watch who we hire. And if the word gets round, and it will, that a couple of detectives came round from District, it can't do any harm at all, see?'

It was an invitation.

Good girl, approved Strapp. This was

the moment the two officers had been hoping for. The rest was a gentle nudge from bright-eyed young Amy Briggs. 'So these Crakes, sir,' said Amy Briggs. 'Not so careful about who they employ?'

'I don't want to say any more, really, but you've got it in one. Be seeing you, then. Any time.'

Alan Barker insisted on accompanying them to the car.

'How'd I do?' said Amy Briggs as they got in. 'You not saying?'

'Good luck with the brothers,' Barker called as they began to move off. 'One more thing. They have what you could call an attitude.'

On the road, Izzy Strapp told his DC she had too: 'Wicked.'

They were sure that the Crakes had something to tell them.

It was in the nature of investigative work that, three minutes later, they were ordered to join a team of officers who were rechecking on the Sheffield stabbings. House-to-house, jogging memories and ensuring that none of the residents had been overlooked. It had been a shockingly bloody incident. The Chief wanted action, and now. 'And the Burngreave depository, Inspector?'

'Priorities, Sergeant,' Tomlinson said. 'The Crakes will keep.'

11

'Let me get a few things straight,' said Mabbatt. 'If you don't mind, sir, that is.'

ACC Dundas had told him to get things moving in the Wolvers investigation. So Mabbatt reinforced the two teams working in Sheffield, cursed the Chief and called on Josh Jowett, he of the unsound mind and unquestionable archaeological expertise. And, a golfer.

'Mind? You're here, the boss, as you might say. Why should I mind? It's about time someone in authority took an interest in that wretch and I call him that advisedly even though he kicked the bucket quite a few years ago. How many, by the way?'

Mabbatt glowered at the frail, tall old man who hovered about a nest of small tables, all littered with sheets of A4 paper covered in a scrawled tiny script; and what looked like badly-drawn pieces of terrain on drawing pads, together with printed charts and a couple of dozen magazines, some open: it looked haphazard, though Jowett trod a confident enough path through the contoured landscape of his sitting room. He was not about to disclose any jot of the information he had received that morning. The post-mortem had been conducted, and the findings were inconclusive; however there was one pointer that might be germane. Tomlinson had sought him out when they were going over the latest reports on the Attercliffe killings. 'I got a short briefing from Professor Edwards at the Pathology Department, sir. He's got a tentative cause of death for the discovery on Monday, which helps, I suppose.'

'Every little,' said Mabbatt. 'He's not one to shoot his mouth off, Edwards. How old is he now?'

'Seventy-eight. And in his prime, so he believes. Very alert, still very dapper, spotted bow tie and all when he popped in at District HQ. You know what he says saw the late Roger Hancock off?'

It was a blow hard enough to splinter a

rib and drive it into the heart.

Brusquely, Mabbatt said to the old man, 'Roger Llewellyn Hancock was probably interred somewhere around eleven years or twelve years ago', Mr. Jowett. Constable Root's report suggested that that was your estimate too.'

'Arthur Root's a good man, but he's a ranker, always will be. And knows his limits, too. Fine chap. Had many like him in my old regiment. Gunners. Battery of twenty-five pounders in Burma. Fine gun.'

'Wouldn't know, Mr. Jowett. Root says you don't have much of an opinion about the theory that this Anglers Kop was a sort of Fort Alamo back a couple of thousand years ago? Sort of massacre of the noble barbarians?'

'Romantic poppycock, Superintendent.'

Mabbatt cast his eyes around the litter of papers and books.

'I see you're quite a reader, by the way? And all these notes — ?'

Jowett's eyes glittered. 'How in God's name, man do you think we get anywhere in my line of research without consulting the available references?'

'You could say the same of us, Mr. Jowett.'

'Exactly! Right on the mark! If I'm to help you excavate Hancock's past, it saves you the bother of doing the spadework, so to speak, my little joke', if you hadn't cottoned on to it?'

'You've quite a way with words, give you that, sir.'

'So where to start?' said Jowett, bustling about his papers, discarding one or another sheets of paper, and kicking over a small heap of unopened small volumes. Mabbatt read a gilt-engraved title: 'Journals of the Yorkshire Archaeological Society, Volume Xiii, as Jowett dithered.

'Start? Let's start with Hancock's crime, sir. What I'd like to get clear first is this: if this colleague of yours was as you described it, a night-hawk, surely it was your duty to report your suspicions the police. Do you have an explanation for this omission, Mr. Jowett?'

Jowett smiled. His hollow cheeks and yellowing teeth gave him a sepulchral appearance. 'Superintendent,' he went on, 'I suspected a crime. I reported my suspicions. It could be that I was either disbelieved or held to be merely a spiteful and vindictive rival of a more successful researcher. No action, I was told, could possibly be envisaged without proof postitive.'

'Your were told this by?'

'The then president of the Yorkshire Archaeological Association, since deceased. Not a man I knew at all well during his lifetime. In fact I was never formally introduced to him, now I think back on the matter.'

'So you informed him, rather than the police, of your — your, what, your conviction that Hancock was a thief?'

Jowett nodded. 'Not by letter. Nor e-mail. The latter was not in such common use ten or twelve years ago as it is today, of course. But I did not wish to leave any written or electronic footprint, Superintendent. I made a telephone call from a public phone box to the late Sir David Ashworth.'

'You phoned, then. And your evidence

that a crime had been committed?'

'In your parlance, hearsay. And, again in your lingo, circumstantial evidence. Deduction, too, and no good it did me. None of it capable of substantiation. And eminently deniable, of course.'

This was leading nowhere, fast. 'Come on, sir. Josh, isn't it?'

Josh Jowett could be succinct when he wished. He rapped out his beliefs and the known facts in quick time. An old friend, Tobias Simmonds, had told a few more friends of a wonderful find on a piece of derelict land in Cadeby, only a few miles from where they sat now. It had been a settlement long before the Romans came, for the surrounding fields were rich, so rich that they were listed with a commendation in the Domesday Book. Simmonds hadn't rung Josh Jowett directly, but it would have been natural for him to be included in the round of calls.

'I was out on that Wednesday evening, a minor social affair. By the time I got back, Tobias had passed away, so I learned the next day.'

'Yes?'

Jowett had pieced it together quickly. One pot had been found, intact, as he had told Arthur Root; and stoppered with a couple of copper coins, to mislead a finder as to its contents. Simmonds had left the pot where it lay, so that experts could make a scientific examination of the ground before removing it. Somehow, so Josh had learned, another had gone — that same night — and looted the cache. Soon after dawn, the museum's two numismatics specialists arrived to find a hollow, and, on scraping away the disturbed earth, one solitary denarius from the time of Diocletian, which meant nothing at all.

And was Hancock one of those who had been joyously told of the discovery? The question was unanswerable, of course. 'See that, yes, Josh.'

Mabbatt was Joe now, in turn. 'Next, how did I come to suspect Hancock? Well, naturally, we turned to one another, our small circle of enthusiasts — Hancock included — and asked ourselves who was the thief. I could swear in court that I saw Roger Hancock smirk. There was a truly unpleasant knowingness about him as he looked you in the eye. I'd seen the look a dozen times on the course: got one over you, haven't I?'

'And, Josh? Hearsay, you mentioned?'

'He was a boozer. And he drank in the noisier and more garish of the public houses. I heard at second hand only, I have to admit, and not from a source that would make a credible witness in a court of law. Rather a low-life. You will not be surprised when I tell you that Hancock was loose in his cups. He could not help hinting that his day had dawned, his particular cup had run over and not with lager either. Hints, but the word 'pot' came through more than twice.'

Mabbatt could see how Josh Jowett was no man to tackle ill-educated locals. Everything was against him, accent, diffidence, a half-accusation maybe that he could not follow up since he would have no skill in interrogative techniques, for all his pedagogical experience.

Mabbatt said as much. 'So he got away

with it at the time. No action by your learned society. Could have spared your pennies on that call.'

Then Jowett surprised him. 'They weren't wasted. The call led, I am quite sure, to the refusal of any further papers from Hancock, which was of course professional death to a scholar. And I also believe,' he said firmly, 'that it led to his subsequent disappearance, and as a chance result of a turn of a JCB's blade has proved, to his mortal demise.'

Jowett looked not unhappy with the outcome.

'So Sir David read the rues aright, then?' Jowett smiled wickedly and said nothing. 'Read the *Guardian* then, Josh?'

It was Mabbatt's attempt at an insult. It misfired.

'Read that rag! Good god, no!'

'There's a copy on your coffee table. By the Nescafe mug.'

'Oh. Yes. But I don't read the damned thing! If you push it aside, you'll see my *Telegraph* underneath. Now that I do read. Are you putting me through some kind of cross-examination concerning my diurnal ingestion of news, Superintendent? And can I offer you a cup of Nescafe? Ready in a jiffy.'

Mabbatt wandered around the large, pleasant sitting room, and settled into a leather clubroom chair, much worn and with real horsehair sticking out from several holes. The room reeked pleasingly of tobacco and — rum, Mabbatt decided. And at three in the afternoon?

There were photographs of Jowett's wedding — posh affair, tails and top hats, the woman small and spindly, Jowett tall and well-set in his youth. 'That was quick,' he told Jowett, wondering what the hell he could say next to get some kind of sense out of his one well-informed but unforthcoming informant.

'I get it for the crossword,' Jowett told him, ignoring his remark. 'Cold milk in the jug. Brown sugar if you want it.'

'Thanks, Mr. Jowett. Now, why don't you tell me about a pot of fairy gold and a Mr. Tobias Simmonds, and your part in subsequent events, as you conjectured them at the time?'

'I thought that you'd never ask.'

Amazingly, they had become friends.

It had happened at some point in the past minute or so.

Josh Jowett had impressed the normally phlegmatic policeman with his outstandingly rugged disparagement of one particularly disturbing element of life in South Yorkshire. Benefits vultures. Or, more properly, asylum-seekers; but however called, they were directed to a vast new redbrick Social Security emporium, one with endless credit for its clients and a willingness to dish out absolutely free all the bounty that a loony set of socialists had assigned them.

Free passes, vouchers, cash by the barrow-load, recently completed flats and houses: all this. 'It's a cornucopia for the shiftless,' Josh Jowett affirmed.

Mabbatt had warmed to him quickly. He flicked the *Guardian*. 'Just the crossword, then?'

'Just that. I use excellence where I find it.'

'So do we. Now, can you tell me anything that will look good in my report to the Assistant Chief? Like, how certain are you about this pot of gold's existence?'

'I can help you there. You see, it's a given that where there's one buried hoard, it's very likely there'll be more.'

'And there were?'

'Within fifty yards. Two more pots. And, to save your time, these finds were properly reported, catalogued and offered to the nation. We may be high-tech moles, Joe, but we are not looters. All is done above board and in daylight.'

'Unlike Hancock, yes. Right, then, will you kindly look into your crystal ball and tell me where that pot of gold might be, Josh? Just an informed guess. Use your experience and intuition, eh? You're a contributor, obviously to your society's journal.'

'Here, see,' Jowett said, drawing with a black felt pen on a pad: JJ. He topped the letters with a line. 'That's how I sign myself. I don't hold with absolute anonymity, but then I wouldn't want to appear egotistical.'

He was gazing reverently at the stack of

leather-bound publications, and in particular at the top one, now open. 'My first piece, forty-two years ago, detailing my best find, and not much of a find at that. Metal-detectors were not much in use then, far too expensive for me. I used first my knowledge, then I applied my intuition, as you recommend now, and scratched around and got lucky. Just a broken earthenware pot with a few dozen *nummi*, scattered around, silvered bronze coins, that is. Small change, but they established the date of a settlement in North Lincolnshire. They establish a trading pattern in the Later Roman Empire. They were not silvered, later.'

'Not valuable? Say, like these gold coins we're investigating?'

Jowett shrugged. 'We come across lots of hoards like these, though 'hoards' exaggerates their importance. People buried their loose change in bad times, what you'd regard as the coins you chuck onto the mantelpiece when the armed gangs came by. If you'd time, you stuck them in a hole in the garden. In an old pot, cracked probably.'

There was more to come. Mabbatt knew a pregnant pause when one was so obviously gestating. 'And they'd leave them?'

'Inflation, Superintendent. Who'd risk their neck going back say twenty years later to dig up a bus fare or two!'

But he did not need clairvoyance to arouse Mabbatt's interest.

'Joe, there's always a trade in gold.'

'And?'

'Find a trader.'

12

There was no need for haste. The corpse had obviously not held life for a considerable time. The dark waters and its animal life had not been kind to the large-bodied man now face down in black mud, where a thread of water from the main flow ran over stark white bone protruding from a rent in his left thigh. Half-a-dozen people had stopped, seeing dramatic events unfold.

'Stand back, all of you,' ordered the young police officer, who had been the first to arrive on the scene, in answer to Control's emergency call.

His colleague, even younger, was directing the shocked finders of the remains to a more sheltered spot out of the cold breeze. The river was not wide here. It narrowed between high wooded banks, where on the northern side a seventy-foot barge was moored, immediately before the modern lock at Sprotborough.

The oldish bargee threw away his cigarette into the dull waters, closely watched by a score of mallards and a pair of Canada geese.

'You kids warm enough?'

The two slim youths in shorts and vests looked back and nodded. Clearly they were not overawed by the presence of a corpse; and not dismayed that they were at the centre of momentous affairs, either.

'Poor bloke's horrible,' said one. 'His face! What was it, rats?'

The police officer did not answer. He indicated a slight rise that was half-sand, half-mud. It was dry enough for them to be seated. 'Won't keep you long. Have a rest. Right, I have to contact your parents. Names?'

His colleague answered another call. 'No, no sign of life. Definitely.' Then he looked at his watch and began to write. 'At o-eight-twenty seven hours, I was ordered to suspend my patrol and proceed to — '

'The Don again,' said Mabbatt, putting the office phone down and re-engaging.

'Keeps cropping up. Strapp? Get me a car.'

★ ★ ★

'Be good, remember!'

Root's mother bustled about, checking sleepover gear and must-have bed favourites. 'Nellie?' she snapped at dreamy Hattie.

'Forgot, Gran!'

The tattered elephant was found and stowed away into the senior Root's shiny new Avensis. He'd explained that he was in process of spending all he could of his son's inheritance whilst he could still get around without a minder.

'We'll miss our train, mum,' grumbled Beth. 'They're going to abandon us in that hell-hole of a spa,' she informed her grandparents. 'Off they'll go, right pleased with themselves.'

'Maybe some charitable folks will adopt you, Beth,' offered her grandmother. 'Someone a bit more soft in the head than your mum is.'

193

'They'll drive you crackers, those two, Gran.'

The twins stuck tongues out at her and smiled calculatedly at one another. 'She rules them with a rod of rhubarb,' said Alf Root. 'They'll come back like two little baa-lambs.'

They had decided to go on the train. The service was slowish, and they had to change at Leeds Central; the bonus was that neither Arthur Root nor his wife had to drive and, as a layer of icing on the cake, the older kids actually requested to travel by rail. Neither parent made any kind of comment.

'No, we're not taking sandwiches,' Ursula had told them both. 'Arthur and I will take lunch at Betty's. It's too damned expensive to waste on you kids, so you get a fiver each and you can disappear for a couple of hours, no three! Right, Arthur?'

'That's more of a ten-pound pay-off, I reckon, mum,' said Beth at once. 'It could be raining. We'd have to go see a film, wouldn't we?'

Tom was an easy-going youth. 'Could. What else could we do?'

'There's a Roman museum,' said Root. 'And there's the Spa.'

'We've been reading about spas in Eng. Lit,' said Beth.

Ursula told Root to get into some gear that suited him, not a tie and white shirt. something colourful with his new designer jeans, right? And bring his bomber jacket. And if it's too hot, tough. She wanted him tall and lean and handsome.

'No shop talk, Arthur. Not today? Nothing nasty?'

'It's all in hand, love. I'm out of the loop. Back to plodding. Yes?'

She came down, a waft of violets before her.

Beth followed afterwards, laced heavily with her mother's scent. Tom had helped himself to Root's Aramis aftershave, the one he used only on special occasions. Well, this was one such. The lad could be put in his place if he made a regular foray into the bathroom cabinet.

'Was that the phone?' Tom said, as they left for the 83 bus that was due any second eighty yards down Acacia Avenue.

'Oh, let it ring,' said Ursula.

Events moved quickly. Procedure had its own inevitability, and as usual, the ACC acknowledged, Mabbatt had organised the deployment of his resources with admirable efficiency. The machinery of a large and well-trained force swung into action with a remarkable speed. Fortunately, there had been a break overnight in the Attercliffe slaying, and a more than a dozen officers could be now be withdrawn from what was not now an investigation, but the subject of formal charges. The husband had been arrested at Manchester Airport, bound, oddly, for Krakow. The arson case was in abeyance, awaiting detailed and what had to be lengthy forensic analysis. Bodies could be deployed, and they were.

'They don't do things by halves on this stretch of river, do they. Superintendent?' the Assistant Chief said cheerfully. Another small tent was being set up behind fluttering blue and white tape as the tall, wide-hipped young pathologist bent to her work in the black slime. 'Two for the price of one, that's the way it is, right, Joe? Iron Age fort with a one-armed skeleton poking out of the ramparts, and now a floater in the muck not far away.'

It was a good thing that Mr. Dundas had come at that moment, for Mabbatt was about to lose his legendary rag. He might have bawled Tomlinson out for an overzealous desire to get under the foul waters of the Don, had not the cheery ACC arrived just then. Instead, bloody Jacques Cousteau got to play in the water.

'I gather you've got a name, Inspector?'

'Local villain, sir. One Daniel Warburton, aged forty-nine, lived in Hagthorpe, by profession a casual worker at whatever he could get, and formerly a professional boxer. Dr. Anderson passed us his wallet — she was here within an hour of the first call to Control. Two officers are sure we've got the right man. Detective-Constable Newton there says he nicked him last year for an affray outside the Miners' Welfare in Garfield. He knew him by the tattoos on his knuckles — a slight variant on the usual, 'WATCH THIS'!'

The cause of death hadn't been

definitively established, of course, but the pathologist had indicated that severe injuries to the right leg, eight or nine inches above the thigh, would have meant that the inevitable blood-loss would very soon result in death. 'Looks crushed, sir. Pulped, more like.'

'And the weapon?'

'The divers aren't hopeful, not after what the bargee told us, but as you know, it's procedure. I — er, I brought my gear along. If you'd excuse me?'

'Commendable, Inspector,' the ACC told him. 'Don't you get nervy, down in the dark?'

'Love it, sir.'

The three-man team who were searching the immediate environs of the river, taking in a twelve-metre stretch, had not been surprised at his appearance in wet-suit and mask. A burly sergeant suggested discreetly that he check yet again on his air-supply. 'Just routine, sir?'

The black waters engulfed them.

The two joggers were on their way home. They had been bursting with information when the first members of the Criminal Investigation Department had arrived, but they had not much to give. The bargee was a find, though. It wasn't the first corpse he had seen in the Don. Mabbatt had arrived as he was ready to talk. Two cigarettes in rapid succession, then Ben Tallis was cautiously forthcoming.

'I reckon he was pushed along the bed, Superintendent. Nothing's certain, but he'd get caught on the mud here after a pulse upstream had gone through. We all know the currents are tricky in the river proper. You get a couple of big boats going down to the bypass canal here at Sprotborough falls that can push a strong bow-wave ahead. Here it's like a capillary, so he'd get swirled, like, off the bed and maybe float a bit. Anyway, that's how I see it. You've got to think about heavy propellers and discharges at locks all the way up to Sheffield as well. It's a considerable body of water, like.'

'So, a lot to go on, Joe,' said Dundas. 'Lots of possibilities.'

The case could be cracked wide open at once, given the right indicators.

Establishing the cause of death led directly to a positive result in most cases. A hefty gash in the head would be a good start for a police officer like Mabbatt. A couple of bullet-holes would be prime; and a good-sized crater from a close-range shotgun blast pretty well the acme. Evidence of a beating-up would do. Failing that, broken limbs might suggest that the corpse had been hurled onto a handy large metal structure, or a chunk of masonry.

The pathologist was still poking around in the mud.

'I thought we'd have DCI Turnbull as Co-ordinator, sir.'

The vital task of bringing together the scientific support team's findings with that of the investigative branch was only a part of the enquiry; the comparing of statements had to be done with the utmost diligence. For the purpose, Mabbatt had chosen his most experienced next in line, a man in his mid-fifties who enjoyed sifting, collating and building the flow chart of events they would need. Detective Chief Inspector Turnbull was a taciturn man who wished, secretly, that he had trained for accountancy.

'Turnbull, good choice,' said the ACC. 'Once you know the victim's name, then it's the juggernaut grinding on, and he does drive it well, Joe.'

'I've ordered all case officers to meet in the Incident Room daily, starting tomorrow, sir. Afternoons. Four. I'd appreciate your being there for the first session.'

ACC Dundas smiled at him. 'Oh, yes? We'll see. Now, two deaths, Joe. The media's going to say it if we don't. There's no such thing as coincidence, right?'

'Never, Mr. Dundas. Belongs with wishful thinking and UFO's.'

Death and gold. The river and a ravaged corpse.

No trained police officer gave any credence to what journalists present as the mysterious workings of fate, with the implication that they knew more than they could disclose. Things were what they were, to the total pragmatists of the investigative branch of the law. The journos were present by now, had been for some time, and not patiently. Tomlinson again, said Mabbatt to himself. He deserved it. Dr. Jane Anderson came to join them.

'Dr. Anderson!' welcomed Dundas. 'I can see that this wretched industrial mud hasn't helped you — made quite a mess of your overalls. I expect there'll be coffee brewing in the support van. Will you join us?'

She was sorry. Her boss wanted her back soonest. She would make it brief, she said, and she did. 'All I can tell you today is that the remains are those of a mesomorphic middle-aged male now considerably overweight, and of course very dead. You will observe that there are obvious signs of injury to the right leg, also severe cranial damage. It's not possible to say exactly the cause of death, but it's my duty to inform you that you can consider this as a probable homicide. I can ask Professor Edwards to get this one ahead of the queue, Mr. Dundas, but it isn't my decision. Will the Crime Scene Manager be ready soon to accompany me to the mortuary?'

They watched the quiet progress of the retinue, a sombre affair.

'Anything to go on yet about this character? No one to fit the frame?'

'Too many, sir. A string of convictions, nothing too serious. Served a couple of short sentences for assault. He'd been a pro boxer, known to have taken bribes, hence he lost his licence when he was still a comparatively young man. He went into bare-knuckle game and did some enforcement work for the loan sharks in Manchester and Sheffield, but that's not to say he hasn't got others looking for his blood. Then he took up cage-fighting, we believe. He was a dedicated alcoholic, maybe into drugs too. His personal life got into a mess, of course, but we're looking at it from every angle.'

Dundas seemed to be considering the inquisitive geese quite closely.

Then he said, 'There are deep and violent passions swirling below the surface here. The dirty old Don. I'm told it can be treacherous. My guess is that all is not what it seems.'

He paused. 'By the way, one thing

before I take myself off, Superintendent.'

'Welcome your advice, as always, Mr. Dundas.' And then he utterly confounded Mabbatt.

'Don't look for a black swan, Joe.'

If he was bewildered, it didn't show, as he attempted to decipher what might be a profound and wise comment on the course of the investigation from a man who had worked in arcane branches of the security services for years as some kind of spook. Clearly, it wasn't a quite literal injunction to avoid seeking out what — a bleeding black swan?

Experience came to his aid.

'Thank you, sir. I shall keep that firmly in mind. At all times.'

He decided to tackle the louts of the media himself.

It was without any surprise at all that they were already well briefed.

'Morning, sir!' yelled a kid from the local TV station. 'Would this be Warburton the cruiserweight, got done for diving, big betting syndicate stuff — I got a text just about him — do I tell the viewers, 'Dirty Dan Done at Don'?'

'No!' yelled the mascara'ed old hack. '*I tell my readers that!*'

'Plagiarising yet again, Lily,' sighed a chubby TV reporter. 'You're welcome luvvie. I'll think of something else to chill the old ladies' chilblains. Give our viewers a quote, Mr. Mabbatt?'

'A quote, now? I might have one for you.' He paused and pointed downriver. 'We are dealing with a major incident. At this time, I am not looking for, repeat, *not* looking for any black swans.'

⋆ ⋆ ⋆

The investigation took an unlikely turn because of Freddie.

'Four o'clock, right here.' Ursula told her two older children.

They had chosen to sit — the parents — on a comfortable enough bench at the top of Montpelier Hill, dedicated to someone's life-long companion, a dog called Frankie that had passed away in 1997, so the plaque read. 'Right here, Frankie's place,' she went on. 'Train's at half-past, gives us plenty of time, but don't be late.'

'And what will you be up to Mum?'

'Shopping,' she told Beth. 'Then Betty's. After that I don't know, but I'll think of something, don't you worry.'

Tom would have preferred to be with his dad, but as usual he went along. The day was warm, with enough of a breeze to stir the sultry air. Cloud hung about, yet the sun struggled to come through Beth would be full of fantasies and would tease him unmercifully. Life. 'Spend a lot of dad's money, Mum. See you!'

They were gone. 'There, Arthur,' she said, pointing to a row of real shops in their leafy triangle, shops with smallish windows in dark greens and gold scrolling and old, old carvings. 'Wait here. I know your attention span when it comes to shops.'

Root determined that the credit card would stay in his wallet, if it was humanly possible; however Ursula had hurriedly explained that this was the exact shop she'd been looking for, where all the rich bimbos in North Yorkshire's golden triangle discarded their designer gear to the needy. This was a very upmarket Scope shop. 'Oh, I can't wait! Stay put!'

'I'll be here, love.'

Root was more interested in a much smaller and comparatively down-market shop with a battered green awning. Old coins beckoned him. A tray of worn and misshaped rings told of hard use and generations of ownership; and here was a tray of fossils — Robin Hood's Bay sprang to mind, a delight when a kid with a small hammer and a knowledgeable adult who could, and would, tell him everything there was to know about trilobites. The prices were in code. That was the old way. The cost of a fairly rare and much desired item was disclosed only when the collector's need was aroused. He was not left alone for long.

'Arthur, I've got to have it! It's such a luscious tarty red!'

Ursula was tugging at his hip pocket just as he was entranced by a small, old trinket-box artfully open to hint at the contents — just one silver chain showed on the key. Clever, of course. It was essential to know what was on the concealed part of the chain.

'It's split too!'

Ursula physically manhandled him across the threshold, where an elegant brace of slim fashionably-dressed middle-aged ladies, their bespectacled gaze firmly on him. Then her. 'Now what have you seen, dear!' the nearer one called, almost bird-like, high and gleeful.

'Something nice in our window?' chimed the other.

Ursula croaked, 'Red — the red — what size is it?'

'Yours!' shrilled the one who reminded Root of a starling. 'Try it! It's just come in. You must!'

She did. 'Arthur!' she called from behind a bright blue curtained area. 'It's dead right, oh, see — wait, the zip won't — It will!' She got help. 'It does!'

'What shall we charge you? It is a Lorelei Blue, sweetie, worn only once — '

'At the Knaresborough Hunt Breakfast Ball!'

'I've got to have it. Salsa!'

He paid, she resumed her jeans and top, and with a huge smile on her face,

Ursula stammered out thanks for the privilege of paying more than Arthur Root thought possible towards a charity he heartily approved of; and by the time they reached Betty's he was in a glow of (donatory) self-pride. They ordered lunch. It was the coin shop that was the crux, though. But that was later.

Harrogate had many charms, the best, for Arthur Root being the wonderfully refurbished Royal Hall. Twelve million, a good chunk of it Lotto money, had gone into its lapus lazuli, its gold and red plush and glittering chandeliers; and generally making up for the many years of disuse and neglect. There was to be a concert in the evening, and it seemed unlikely that they could get a peek into the hall, since a rehearsal was in progress; but the plump ladies who guarded the lobby were impressed by his upright bearing and stern, long reddened face. Secretly, they took him for an off-duty soldier, a tough specimen from one of the infantry camps out Catterick way. Ursula, they barely glanced at.

Only when they saw Beth and Tom

staring fixedly at the window of the shop with the green awning did they get a hint that the day had turned against them. As if to confirm it, a light spattering of rain began, and now Arthur Root was glad of his bomber jacket. Without thought, he put it around Ursula's shoulders as she asked what was the matter. She grabbed his arm tight. 'Tom! Beth! Look at me, you two. What's wrong?'

'It's dead like Auntie Grace's she says,' said Tom, speaking for once for his over-verbose sister. 'That gold coin, the little one.'

Root drew them into the shelter of the porch. Beyond, a scruffy-looking bald man in a green roll-neck with ponytail and beard to match looked back at them. He nodded amiably enough. A customer was a prospect, whatever age or shape or form. 'Beth? Look, our train goes in not much more than half-an-hour. Can we talk then?'

'Dad, have a look at it. Please. She had one when I was a kid. I was rooting in the front bedroom when I shouldn't, you know how you do when you're just little and you want to dress up?'

'She had it from that rotten Danny, didn't she!'

Ursula and Arthur Root looked at one another. He pressed her arm gently. She knew that he would now take over. Grace's son had had flattened Danny Warburton only recently.

'All right, Beth. She had what, a gold coin? Gold?'

'Just like that! A wolf with two kids, they're Romulus and Remus, Dad, they were brought up by a she-wolf, didn't you know!'

'They reminded her of the twins, Dad,' said Tom. 'Must have triggered off a memory. The mind's like that.'

Root glanced at his son and nodded. 'Yes, lad. Foreign territory, the past. You don't know what lies hidden. Beth? This coin. Tell me about it.'

'I can see it now, Dad. On a gold chain. I put it on, and Auntie Grace told me off. She said she shouldn't have kept it — she was crying. And she said she'd chuck it away, oh, Mum!'

It wouldn't keep, Root decided. He

nodded back to the man in the shop and turned to his small and now disturbed family. 'Just wait with the kids, Ursula. I won't be long. We'll get the next train. Beth, thanks. But put it out of your mind now. Right?'

The owner wasn't particularly troubled, Root saw. No doubt he assumed that there had been a dispute about whether or not the smart-looking kid with the other one, the lad, should have a chance to spend her pocket money on a whim. He had no hopes for a sale. Dad looked a bit grim.

'I'm sorry to have to ask this, sir,' said Root, 'but maybe you can help me? Can I see that coin, please — yes, that tray, top and second left. Not a big coin. Maybe I'll be interested some time.'

He elicited the information he was after in a couple of minutes, leaving a numismatist totally unimpressed by his deception. The dealer could recognise an official and purposeful enquiry when he heard one. There was no reason to hold back, so Root learned all that the dealer was prepared to tell him, which was enough. For now. Beth was right, as usual when it came to literature. The noble profile on the obverse was that of Constantine the Great.

'His old man snuffed it at York, on campaign, sir,' said Jeremy Tolchard, a name Root had noted from his accreditations. 'That would be Constantius One. Now, Constantine the First got the job right away, by acclamation. In AD 337. Fine statue at the Minster. Your daughter — yes? — has her facts right. Clever girl, quite right about the she-wolf. Not the most attractive of foster-mothers, but you see, it's good propaganda to say you're in a direct line from the founders of Rome. Makes you legit. I can do it for, three-fifty?'

Root took away only the dealer's business card.

It was a chink of light. Danny Warburton hadn't gone to the small terraced house in Gritmarsh to try to mend a rift or scrounge a few pounds for the evening's beer. *Gary, now. And Grace.*

'All's well,' he told his family. 'Good

thinking, Tom. Beth, it's not your problem. Let's make a run for the station, it's bucketing down.'

Then call CID, for this was much more than a domestic.

Jeremy Tolchard decided to make one or two calls, to make sure that all he was doing was also legit.

13

Gary Brand knew it would be his father in the river as soon as she told. him about the discovery just downstream of the golf club. He blocked it out, just as he had blocked out so many scenes of rage and blood. 'No, not heard anything about it,' he told her. 'Been busy, seeing to a load of magic carpets for the Khans.'

'Took your time, Gary.' She wanted to hear about it; and she wanted to be with him. The van was parked beside a small Fife harbour, not far from a busy fried food shop, where he'd bought haggis and chips and Iron Bru. 'Feeding your face, then When do I see you?'

They talked for a half-hour, with Gary conscious that top-ups last for only so long. And then she was called away, but not before she'd said that the heaving bar was full of talk about yet another corpse being found, some old bloke, big, and Phil Church had been talking to the tall

215

inspector who'd come about the skull and bones at the Kop, gruesome. 'Name? No, didn't catch that. Murdered, so they say. Right by the lock at Sprotborough, got to go, Gary, it's all happening here, creepy Charlie's in a state, and ring me in the morning, you hear? I'm worth another top-up, aren't I?'

★ ★ ★

'That face of his when they lifted the sheet off of him! Stark white, and him always red with that big nose of his flattened. But where's our Gary? I mean, it's three days, and Mr. Khan just says he's doing a round of deliveries up in Scotland. What's got into him, not ringing. I don't know if he even knows his father's dead, do I?'

That was when they'd made her drink whisky in her tea.

Arthur Root had flatly refused to allow his wife to accompany him to her friend's house. 'Beth's had a shock. I can cope with Grace, and besides I'm bringing her back here when I've seen the DCI.'

Ursula didn't trouble to argue. 'We're going to Grace's. You kids, feed yourselves. You Beth move into the twins' room. I'll tell her we're on the way Arthur.'

There were a dozen calls awaiting him when they'd got back to Acacia Avenue. Florrie O'Brien petulant about her Singer. Josef Grzebieniowski had news of a tearaway Romany waif. Sarah giggling incoherently, with Sue. Josh Jowett thought the back six might suit, say, Wednesday. Sergeant Strapp requested a return call, and so Arthur Root learned that Danny Warburton had died, probably in the murk of the Don; and that Mabbatt wanted a word, soonest.

'Tried a mobile number we've got down, Arthur. Lost your charge?'

The eighth and ninth calls were from Grace Brand. All she said was that she hoped they were all right. She sounded as though she spoke from a hollow place encased in ice. When they got to Orchard Close, they found the house in darkness, and it took two or three minutes before they could get a response. It had been horrific, they learned. Naturally, Inspector Tomlinson and Miss Briggs had been courteous and kind. But they needed a confirmation of the dead man's identity, and if she could possibly manage it? — say, when she had got herself together. 'Anyway, it's over,' she said to her two closest friends, who were stricken by their failure to be there when Grace needed them. There was no one else, really, she could call on. Some friendly acquaintances; one or two elderly neighbours who might have been called on, but weren't. 'They were all scared of him. I didn't want them upset. They think he did it. Our Gary.'

'No, Grace. No one jumps to any conclusions. They've only to look at Gary's record to know he's solid. And the way he went to the station before setting out, that has to say he's straight with us. Put it out of your mind. Do you know where he is? I want to help him, you know that.'

She had stopped shivering. Warburton was a thing of the past.

Root considered. 'Would you tell me

what Danny was after, Grace? When he came on Monday? The more I know, love, the better I can help the lad. See, I think I know, really — is it to do with that gold coin and chain that Beth saw all those years ago? In the little front bedroom?'

Grace froze. Her hand clenched hard on Ursula's firm hand.

'That rotten thing! I should have thrown it out years back!'

Root had explained that he must question Grace. She was against it, but she saw that the practicalities of policing made it necessary.

'Arthur's looking after Gary. But it looks like it all sort of ties up, so if you can bear to talk?'

It was harrowing for all of them. Nothing hardened you to violence against women, thought Root. Grace began.

'Nine years back.' It was a cold, February day. 'He came in bellowing, just as always, full of ale. I knew what he wanted right away.' There was a long wait, and it took shape in their minds, the assault and the alcoholic half-apology that was mostly self-justification.

'I tried to slam the door on him. People say they don't know their own strength. He knew his.' After he'd finished with her. Danny Warburton had fished in his pocket and he said he wanted to give her a proper present now they were back together, man and wife. They'd been loving one another, he declared, belching fumes into her pinched face. 'Must be worth a thousand, at least' he told her. 'I had it set myself, got a jeweller to drill it and find me a bit of chain — and, mark you, all gold right enough. Charged me another tenner for just the catch. See, it's on a spring.'

'And Gary? He knew?'

'Never. Lucky he was out. Footballing. In the park, down at the rec with his mates. I don't know what he'd have done if he'd seen his dad in that state.' She flared momentarily. 'Gary didn't stand for it Monday, did he?'

Arthur Root finished telling it. 'Did he find it, Grace?'

She nodded wearily. 'And one or two other bits I'd kept. There was a cameo brooch from Grandma Cotton.' And a very ordinary silver bracelet that Gary had bought her from his savings one Christmas when he was working as a newspaper delivery boy. 'He took the lot.' She regained her composure then. 'Didn't he always?'

And, no, she was better now they'd been. So Beth could have her own tiny room back, and Grace Brand would wait for her son to ring. Arthur Root dropped her off and headed for the great new tower of concrete and crystal that was the home of the Criminal Investigation Department. He made a brief call before he set out, though.

★ ★ ★

On Sunday Root was called to the first sixteen hundred hours session in the big open-plan floor space that was now the incident room. An hour before it opened, Superintendent Mabbatt and DCI Turnbull had taken him over his written report of the events beginning with Tolchard's identification of the Romano-British fourth-century aureus; and the history of the coin that the deceased, Warburton, had allegedly stolen from the house in Orchard Close. Grace had not yet been asked to make a statement, but one would be needed soon. 'A bad end, but then he was a bad bastard,' remarked Mabbatt. 'We agreed that last night, Root. Right?'

It had been a close examination, but, fortunately, not a long one. He was able to join Ursula in a late meal.

'So we needn't bother Mrs. Brand again just yet, sir?'

Turnbull, not a man to voice opinions strongly, thought Root, agreed.

'Tomorrow will do,' Arthur Root heard, with relief.

How she could have put up with a bastard like Warburton for more than five minutes was beyond him, Mabbatt said, but the DCI was right. Her few facts would fit into the general mosaic when they'd looked into, amongst other matters, the old pug's connections with the local gambling syndicates — he'd called them 'bleeding sharks', and the words stuck in Root's mind, conjuring up images of swirling dark water and

Danny's terrible injuries, and how the pathologist thought that he might have crawled from some scene of horror to the seeming safety of the stinking Don, as he sat amongst a crowd of large and fit young men and women, all waiting for a tense, eager Superintendent of Detectives to start the proceedings.

'The Assistant Chief Constable has sent his apologies,' Mabbatt began. 'He wished to be here, but he'll certainly be with us tomorrow at this time. So will I.' There were a few smiles, not many. Mabbatt glowered around the sunlit room, found all was respectful attention and continued, 'We could be looking at two murders, not one, as you all will have gathered from your briefing notes. When I've done, Mr. Turnbull will explain how we will liaise and coordinate the investigation soon, but a few facts first.'

He was concise, logical and impartial. Warburton had lived the life his physical prowess had fitted him for. Fame and considerable fortune had come his way, and so had marriage, a home and a child. He chose to misuse and then abuse all of these. You have the pathologist's findings, and you know that weapons of some kind are involved, and must be sought. Certain information had very recently come to our attention, which seemed to indicate that there could be a causal link between the death of Roger Llewellyn Hancock — and refer to your notes again, please — and the deceased, Warburton. Item One, a gold coin. Two, the existence, and this had not yet been established as a fact, though it would be diligently investigated, that a hoard of ancient treasure may have surfaced in the locality. Warburton's known links with the gambling fraternity, which suggested the possibility of debt and hence a need for immediate funds.

'This is, so far, a theory. Before you hear any more, I want to say that we have no suspicions about any person or persons being involved with or responsible for Warburton's death. You will see that he was involved in a domestic dispute with his son. That's Gary Brand, who long since disowned him. Mr. Brand has not yet been interviewed, but that will be taken care of shortly.'

Root's long frame stiffened. To hear Gary's name said aloud in this context before so many men and women, some of whom he had known for years, was suddenly a paralysing and literally a breathtaking experience.

Yet Mabbatt hadn't given him a glance — for which he was grateful — before he went on to sketch the lines of enquiry that the phalanx of investigative officers would undertake: bookies, boxing promoters and their illegal counterparts who put men in a cage to smash one another into wrecks; archaeological experts, professional and, like Josh Jowett, amateur; pubs and clubs, a particular storage depot, a golf club, the residences near the lock, all would be checked. Informers, suspected drug dealers and similar low-lifes would be robustly interrogated. There would be more, naturally, Mabbatt explained, and when Root looked at his watch he found that only twenty minutes had gone by from start to finish. 'You can ask questions when Mr. Turnbull's done,' he said. 'Right?'

'Yes sir.' Mabbatt had been brief, but

he had spoken with authority and zeal, if not an infectious sense of a sheer, brutal lust for the hunt. 'Yes, Mr. Mabbatt!'

They knew Turnbull would be thorough but not concise. He disliked modern gadgets, never putting on a video show or even an old-fashioned projector display. He always produced handouts, meticulously prepared.

He was not a natural communicator, yet he did set their minds at rest immediately on a point that had caused quite a lot of argumentative discussion since the media had put out the Superintendent's gnomic remark at Sprotborough Lock.

'Thanks sir. I'll go over now what we've got and tell you of what we're going to do. First, though, I'd like you to know how much I was impressed by the Superintendent's intellectual appraisal of the criminal investigation — or, as we've heard, possibly investigations. Yes, I find myself inspired by the notion that we are not in pursuit of that rarest of birds a black swan.' Mabbatt's face was set. It showed nothing but alert approval. There were maybe four or five in the audience sufficiently experienced and intelligent enough to — maybe — sense a little of his discomfort; for he had become, unanimously amongst the media, a soothsayer, one whose truth could be interpreted, if you could but see into the heart of the matter. And as yet he didn't know what Mr. Dundas had been on about with his sodding black swan. Someone could just conceivably, right now, be in process of detecting a false note in his barmy pronouncement to the kid with the camera and the mouthy made-up hag from the Sheffield paper. Yet a senior officer of proven ability was lauding him and the bloody black bird, all in one!

'Yes,' he heard, 'Mr. Mabbatt knows full well that what Taleb put so pithily. In essence, it is impossible in advance to devise a strategy for the totally unpredictable. Yet, when it comes, we acknowledge that it is so. And we look for what's there.'

By the time he had explained the central thesis of the Lebanese-American financial trader, Nassim Nichol Taleb, there was a glazed look developing on the faces of most of the police officers. He cited the rogue trader who had brought down a centuries-old London bank, a tsunami that came out of calm seas to kill two hundred thousand Asians, a jehadist strike with vast jet aircraft against great financial towers, and a bride struck by lightning as the confetti danced around her. 'Yes, but once we accept that the rarities of such an event is necessarily inconsequential, we can make progress,' Turnbull was saying enthusiastically. 'It lies beyond the range of normal human prediction. And Mr. Mabbatt recognised that it was so at once! Yes, at once! A black swan would be a total aberration so far as this enquiry is concerned. Right, Superintendent?'

Mabbatt allowed a slight nod of his big, solid chin.

'I'll get a bit of background in now,' said Turnbull. 'Philosophy is one thing, but it's the nitty-gritty that gets results, am I right? Warburton's house in Hagthorpe, Detective Constables Drewitt and Singh. Let's have a brief report to start the ball rolling. Stand, please.'

Two detectives who would have preferred to be on another enquiry altogether, had searched the place. It was, they reported, a shit-hole. The place was infested with blue-bellied flies. The search had extended to the mattress, and no, no gold coin from the reign of Constantine the First.

'Gold. We will find it, and I will now explain how.'

It took Turnbull almost two hours to do just that. Arthur Root wondered if he would see any part of the ongoing investigation. Peripherally, he might be involved. There were ideas stirring in his mind. But it would be best to leave the fieldwork to the experts. They had been fired up; then pumped up; and now they wanted to get into the action.

'That's it for today,' finished Turnbull. 'Black swans are out.'

'If I see one, I'll shoot the bugger,' a burly old CID sergeant said as they left. 'Anyway, I don't reckon much to Yanks.'

His mate said he could say the same about the Lebanese. They agreed that this Zaleb bloke hadn't been Down Under.

The ACC sent for Mabbatt. Over cups of weak tea, he told him to get along to the golf club. 'You'll have to use that head-on technique of yours, Joe. And before long. Do like that fortuitous JCB blade did. I recommend it. Dig. Like a steel blade, Superintendent. Yes?'

★　★　★

Monday morning, Gary was turning out of a small industrial estate on southern fringes of Edinburgh when a patrol car gently moved ahead of him.

Trouble. And he was alone, on unfamiliar terrain.

'There is something wrong, then?'

'If you lock the van, you can ride with us. Our inspector thinks it's better he has a talk with you himself. We can't insist. But you're used to the way things go, officially that is. All right, Gary?'

'No sweat,' said the second man, older, a hard beaky face and a thick accent that was surely from farther west: Glasgow, no doubt. 'Three minutes to the station, that's all?'

It was a squalid suburb of high tenements and small pub fronts.

'I'll get straight to it, Gary,' said the inspector. 'It's bad news.'

'So mum had to go to the morgue, when, two days ago — by herself?' he said, his voice breaking at the thought of his mother, alone, with that grisly last duty to perform for a man who had so betrayed her and for so long. 'I should have — '

'Not alone, I can tell you that much, Gary.'

He was told that he would be more fully informed of all matters relevant to the fatality on his return home. Meanwhile, did he believe that he was fit to drive, given that he had received such tidings so recently.

'I'll get through on my mobile. My mum, see.'

He could recollect now that the officers who had stopped him had also looked him up and down with he knew now was a most cautious appraisal. They were men accustomed to hard times. Given any hint that he might be full of guilty fear then their attitude would have been quite different.

Before he could turn to go, the inspector indirectly confirmed it. 'We had to run a check,' he said. 'Routine. I was Army before I joined the force, so I know a bit about it. We heard about you taking over the Warrior cannon when your mates were hit. Made an impression in the right places, that's all I can say. Now go home, and remember you've a guardian angel looking out for you. And good luck, laddie.'

It was too much to absorb immediately.

'Mum,' Gary said to himself. 'Then Josie.' He would tell them both he needed them.

14

Arthur Root reviewed his day. He had a four-year-old on each knee and a zany CBBC cartoon about a laid-back scruffy dog and his brainless pack on the new Panasonic widescreen; Beth was helping her mother in the kitchen, and Tom had a soccer practice, so he wasn't back yet. Before, attending the mandatory meeting, he'd shown the uniform in Gritmarsh, taking care to vary his routine.

Rosie from Mr. Chang's superstore, as he called it, had chided him for not arresting the gippo kids or chasing up the teenagers who had resumed skateboarding in the small mall. Drawing deeply on a Marlboro Lite, she had asked how Grace was bearing up now Danny was gone. Well enough, she was assured. And then she fitted another small part into the jigsaw puzzle. 'Bookies'll miss him. He was in for thousands.' That was being looked into, but the other fragment she offered was in his own orbit. 'Cheeky little bugger falling over his nicked trainers, told me he'd like a cig too, and his mates but in foreign. Handsome lad, he'll be. Fancies himself, with that medal round his neck. You found Changie's trolleys, Arthur?'

Root had stored away the fragment. *Kid with a medal on his neck.* It could mean something or nothing. Josef, now, he'd been in touch and so far Root had been too busy to return his call. The twins broke in, wanting to switch knees. Beth told him to make sure they washed their hands, and Tom came in, lithe and glowing, bursting to tell him that he'd be playing as a roving left back on Saturday, and could his dad make it? 'No, son. I'm caddying for the Major, remember? The Pro-am-am-am?'

There would be the afternoon round, a shotgun start that the Major, as Captain of Wolvers Golf Club would fire off. Afterwards, Mr. and Mrs. Root would attend the evening function, which would be informal dress, very. He had twice seen Ursula stroking the inflammatory charity frock. 'Up, you two. Duggy Dog wants you to wash your hands.'

And all the time he wanted to know about gold and bones, and when Josh would come up with another thread for the gatherers to seize on; Mabbatt had indicated that he might resume his normal duties, with the obvious implication that he was superfluous, at most a minor irritation. Strapp, now. Izzy would keep him up to date. He'd promised as much. So what would they have done, today, what sources of information would they have drained?

There was no call for him that evening.

The good news was that Gary was home.

★ ★ ★

'Well, finally we got here,' Strapp said to Detective-Constable Briggs.

They were here to ask the Crakes what was known about one of their old acquaintances from the bare-knuckle and cage days: Warburton. The sister, Hancock's, had indicated that they were welcome to what they could find. She had been asked if she knew of any archaeological discoveries he might have made; and whether it might be possible that he could have cached any such finds along with his household goods; however, she had not been told that there was a faint possibility that there might be the contents of a Romano-British earthenware pot stashed away, say in a fridge-freezer or a blanket chest. Mrs. Wilcox said she didn't want to know. The Warburton association pushed the level of urgency up a notch. So here they were, before four-acres of old industrial land in a rundown and desolate part of Burngreave. NO ADMISSON, AUTHORISED PERSONS ONLY read a sign in fluorescent green on a disintegrating chipboard kitchen door affixed to a formidable barrier fashioned from rusting corrugated metal sheeting, barbed wire, tangled chain link and ancient iron railings. Beyond, was a jungle of wrecked cars and transport vehicles, with an orange and white double-decker bus at the far reach of the site. Stacked containers had once been adapted for individual storage use, several doors hung. Strapp noticed an oddity. He could see half a rear wheel and panniers. It gleamed amongst the wrecks, a newish, large motorcycle.

'Looks deserted.' Amy Briggs rattled a stretch of chain-link. Three rail-thin dogs appeared, not barking, not chained either, they noted. A bitch, heavy in pup, joined them. She opened her mouth and let out a high call. The dogs fanned out, pack-fashion. The old bitch sat on its haunches. Two sallow cross-German Shepherds watched the officers closely. 'Well, we're not going in there,' said Strapp. 'Not without tasers. Hey! Anyone around?'

He had a huge voice. It boomed around metal sides and caused the dogs to answer at once. The bitch rushed forward, snarling. 'Nice doggie,' said Amy. 'I'll knock the shit out of you if you try anything.'

'Crake! Reuben and Royston Crake! We are police officers, and we want a word. Now!' he roared, just as Amy

Briggs let the siren rip out in the calm, warm air. It echoed back eerily. And out came the Crakes.

Six-foot four or five of hugely over-weight South Yorkshire — a lot of fat hanging below thick leather belts with heavy brass buckles: but a lot of brawn nevertheless. A glance quieted the dogs.

Strapp had said they'd show their credentials. 'You'll be the Crake brothers, right? We've come because you run a storage depot. That's what we want to talk to you about.'

The slightly taller of the two had a wall-eye which split his focusing so he seemed to stare at both Amy and the heavily-pregnant bitch separately yet simultaneously. He was not the spokes-person. 'He's Reuben. I'm Royston Crake, and we're out of that game.'

Strapp made it obvious that he was ready to be awkward. He was big and round, a ponderous authority. Royston weighed up his options. He chose co-operation. No, they weren't running any kind of storage business. It wasn't a paying business, storing gear for months and then finding that half of it had been ditched on you, worth nowt when you looked in. 'And?'

'I want you to check your records, Mr. Crake,' Strapp told Royston. 'I want to know if a Mr. Roger Hancock rented a storage facility from you some years ago. Will you look in your books?'

'Be lucky,' said Royston. 'Long gone.'

'Yuh,' Reuben put in. 'Gone. Burned the buggers.'

'And when was that?' said Strapp. Amy Briggs admired Strapp's timing. 'About when Danny packed in here, would it be?'

He hadn't told her in advance he'd work it that way. But it did work.

Royston shrugged. Reuben agreed. 'Yuh.'

They looked at one another for a moment. It had gone wrong. Reuben gaped and shook his head, trying to claw back his agreement. 'Nah.'

Royston got out, 'Danny, Danny who?'

Too late. Strapp mentioned the names of managers, gyms and venues.

He said he knew for a fact that Danny Warburton was a close associate if not a

239

friend of theirs during the time that he was a fighter. 'In the ring and then after, Royston, when he was kicked out. Stands to reason he'd come to you for a job when he was broke. Look, he's dead. Murdered. Be helpful. I don't want to have to come back, do I?'

''Dead in Dirty Don',' his brother quoted, after a climb down. 'Paper said. He were all reet when he weren't pissed, like, Danny.'

'Shut it, Rube,' he grunted. 'Sacked him, Sergeant. Always summat missing when the punters came for their goods. Never anything much but we had to stand it, give them a few notes, like. Always broke.'

'So when did you see him last, Mr. Crake?'

Royston bristled. 'Ay, don't start thinking anything about us and Danny getting done! I wouldn't drink with him, I told him that years back!'

'And what about Mr. Hancock's goods, sir?' put in Amy Briggs.

'I got rid of any decent stuff to some Paki dealers in Brightside. Renting out 'ouses to their lot.'

It was an impossible request, but it had to be tried. 'Mind if we look around your premises, then, Mr. Crake?'

'No point, is there? What you see is what we got. Recycling, that's what we do. Just old machinery, car wrecks, save what we can sell on. Legit, Sergeant — Sergeant Strapp. Sorry not to 'elp, Miss.'

'Nice bike,' said Strapp. 'You can't be doing so badly here.'

Reuben gaped and Royston said wasn't it and he spent his money the way he wanted, nothing wrong with that? When they were away from the site, Amy said that Reuben was hiding something. 'Course he is,' Strapp told her, rather impatiently. 'I need authority though to get in. And I've nothing to tell the super to make it stick. I can't see they'd have left any loot lying around.'

There would be no pot of gold in this part of once-thriving Sheffield.

'Did they have a decent business — ever? What's your guess?'

'Doubtful.'

'That poor old bitch,' Amy remarked, possibly to herself. Strapp let it pass. Then she said, 'Now what?'

'Maybe we'll get to see that posh golf club again soon.'

* * *

Mabbatt had not been pleased with the ACC's comments after the third liaison meeting. What had seemed to be promising leads had resulted in glitch, nothing, nowt. Tomlinson had called in at the numismatist's shop, accompanied by a senior officer of the North Yorkshire force, naturally. The balding pony-tailed dealer was quite ready to answer their questions. He had checked and re-checked the whole of his stock, in particular the seven gold coins of the period that had interested the lanky cop with the sharp-eyed kid who'd certainly get 'A's' in her GCSE History. 'I can show you valid receipts from reputable valuers or auction houses for all of them,' he said. 'I'm glad I can, given your interest. This is the kind of business that attracts all sorts of people on the edge of the law, I know. But I'm strictly legitimate and of course I'm very careful to obtain a provenance for anything brought in. Now, the coin you're interested in is one I got from an old Harrogate resident's estate. The executors came in — June, the nineteenth — and wanted a price for his collection. They're a well-regarded family. This is my receipt. I was very interested in the *aureus*, naturally. It's not a particularly rare coin, so it's not of a huge value — Constantine's mints produced a lot of them. As for how it came into the possession of the late Mr. Pickles, they're not sure. What I can tell you is that he'd owned it for fifty-odd years, but they think it came on the market from a hoard as far north as York. In those days, it was perfectly legal to buy and sell anything you found — not now. But you'll be aware of the present laws covering treasure trove?'

Tomlinson had made it his business to know. He'd consulted Josh Jowett first, and then the local museum to firm up his knowledge. 'Doesn't take you much further on, then, Inspector, does it?'

It tied off one loose end.

Superintendent Mabbatt was keenly reaching for another.

⋆　⋆　⋆

'Well, I must say you try to make a fella comfortable, Mr. Church,' the Superintendent was saying to the Secretary of Wolvers Golf Club. 'Don't he, Josh? My boss was most impressed when he heard you'd asked me here for coffee and whatnot. I take it the Major can manage to get along, too?'

'Alf's got no notion of time, Mr. Mabbatt,' said Church. 'Others have got to jump to it, but he's got his own internal clock. He did say he thought Arthur was doing a good job, by the way, just come into my mind. And he said that young Gary Brand looked to be in a bit of trouble, so he'd put in a word. Yes, pour it, will you, Josie?'

Mabbatt looked down the scoop in her blouse and told himself that young Gary was lucky twice over. It had been recorded that, amongst the complex relationships that were part of the club's social life, the brisk young lad and the tasty Darfield girl were an item. It had not escaped his notice, too, that the smarmy bastard behind the bar watched her breathlessly.

'Mr. Dundas thought I should have a word about Hancock,' he said baldly. 'Josh here has been very useful, all that expertise of his, that ding-dong that's supposed to have happened out there and didn't. It looks likely that there's a considerable motive, since there could be a stolen pot of gold involved, I'm on the right track, Josh? Yes. So I'll tell you what I know from our sources.'

He did. It amounted to very little.

'Late on parade!' came a great unrepentant roar. 'Brandy, large, Bliss, instanter! Joe Mabbatt, glad you could make it! We're teeing off at two prompt on Saturday — going to be an excellent day's golf — you'll come?' Major Wynne-Fitzpatrick was in full flow. 'Your bobby Arthur Root volunteered to caddy for me you know, decent of him, but then he's a damned fine fella all round, yes? Well he's up to his ears as you know, what with this old pug being found in the river and all, so young Gary Brand's offered instead you know — got him in as a member on his battle ticket. You know, we can do it by the rules, given a good show, unanimous decision after we knocked the damned Boers for six, lost some good men from round here — Spion Kop, where are we with Hancock's bones?'

Root involving himself in CID business? And his protege under Major Wynne-Fitzpatrick's wing? The bloody club was another Vatican.

Mabbatt knew he had to use his interpersonal skills. He repeated his non-news and then put the question he'd come especially to ask — consequent on the information one of his teams had gleaned. 'Well, er, Alf, maybe one of your members could throw a bit more light on just that. You know Josh helped with the archaeological background and these treasure-seekers-detectors that bend the rules, but we want something a bit specialised, like dealing in coins — I think it's a Mr. Jones that could be of assistance. Phil?'

They were both a bit leery, he thought, but they were necessarily constrained to demonstrate a willingness to uphold the Law, good solid citizens that they were: and knowledgeable too in the secret ways of power, locally. Mabbatt had taken pains to investigate Edward Jones's antecedents. He was definitely not a Mason. Scorned approaches, so it was said. Well, he would, wouldn't he? Given his background. 'Ted's been a member here for years, seven, eight,' said Phil Church. 'I suppose there was a bit of a confab when his application came up — ah, don't think we've any kind of prejudice, and if there might have been that's not the case now! Not at all! Why, we've a splendid racial mix here! Three Indian doctors. And a Sikh, what's he — dentist, yes. But Ted? Salt of the earth. He'd be the first to want to help.'

'Quite,' said Josh Jowett. 'Of course.'

'Cheery sort, yes,' said the Major. 'Looks as though he's miles away sometimes, though. Been through it, sometime, I'd say. Alice sets him right. Good sort, that. Bit of a tiger when it came to sentencing fellas too ready to use their fists. Ted, though. Listen to Phil here — no discrimination on racial grounds at Wolvers. That's what the big war was all about, come to think of it. Forgive me, Joe. Old stories, best forgotten, leads nowhere. Thought of something — what you said the other day about these black swans, man — not on a wild-goose chase, are you? Eh!'

Josie Marsden stood immobile well away from the men. Gary would be ringing when she finished, just after nine. What a tale to tell him!

'I want to thank you for your valuable time, gentlemen,' Mabbatt said unctuously. 'I'll bear that in mind, Major. I expect the Assistant Chief Constable would appreciate the thought. Now, if you'll excuse me and Josh, I'd like to have another look at this Kop. I can't help feeling that we haven't got to the bottom of why Hancock should have finished up there — so we'll go see, shall we, Josh?'

'Clues, that's what we're looking for, Joe. Now the JCB's gone, we can tread over the ground. Nosey lot,' he said, indicating a foursome who'd looked their way. 'Still, we all like a good murder, don't we?'

'We've not got much farther in finding who did it. No result with your informant, this boozer Staples you put us onto. Went out with a ruined liver five years back. But we're getting bits and pieces in. All adds up.'

'I trust it will Joe,' Jowett said sincerely. 'In classical times, law enforcement was in the hands of men just like you. I could show you one or two accounts of the Roman justice system at work, if you like?'

'What I like is you talking about Hancock. And this fight, the one Root said was like the Alamo, but didn't happen. I'm listening. On with it, Josh.'

'Spion Kop is most definitely an integral part of the mythology we're looking at. Misnamed, as you've gathered. Doubly so, since it pre-dates Anglo-Saxon time. The Alamo outcome is more relevant however. You'll get the idea when I say that this Saunders-Roe heir put a couple of hundred yokels in replicas of Roman armour and Britons' bearskins, or whatever his advisers told him the Coritani dressed up in when they went to war. He had ballistae and wild asses made, trenches dug, and a wooden fortification established on the summit — what, Joe?'

'Trenches. I'll come back to them. One thing, though, you'd talk quite a bit about all this to your mates here at the club?'

Not for long, Mabbatt learned. Only a very few who had an especial fondness for re-fighting ancient battles. And who, in particular? Maybe Mr. Jones, 'cos of his professional interest, perhaps?

'You could say that, yes. He followed the route of Paulinus Suetonius's sweep North against the Brigantes — a most daring campaign, considering the fact that he had a nationwide insurgency at his back, Boudicca on the rampage, you see — ah! I get carried away, I know.'

Mabbatt smiled back. Fortitude, Joe lad. 'We all can, Josh.'

'Ah, yes. But you were asking about trenches, I recall. A clue? Not saying, are you. All right, back to the Romantic. Did I say he was something of an exhibitionist? And a bit. He got himself painted blue where it showed and dressed up as a Coritanian chieftain, spear and longsword and all, and finished it off with his full Masonic regalia on top. Then he headed a procession from the Hall to the battle-lines. All the local dignitaries turned out, had to really. It made quite a show, according to the contemporary newspaper reports. Then it all got rather out of hand, since he'd had a special ancient brew made up, again on the information from his Oxford dons. There were twenty-four hogsheads of what they called mead in the central keep of the fortification, and that proved an incentive to attackers and defenders alike. The Roman yokels didn't trust their Ancient Briton mates to save them any, so they got stuck in before the time the event was scheduled to begin, which was for two o'clock prompt.'

'Dear god,' said Mabbatt in something like awe. 'A South Yorkshire Saturday afternoon fixture. With free beer. Special Brew, was it? Bloody rocket fuel! How did it finish?'

'The tally was thirty-two broken legs and arms. They didn't count concussions. Too difficult to diagnose, given the circumstances.'

'Who won? The blokes in the trenches?'

'Joe, we both know what happens to battle casualties in a real war. I was there once. There are always perfectly adequate ready-made graves, that's what you're weighing up, isn't it.' Obviously, from Mabbatt's narrow-eyed searching of the disturbed ground, it was. 'Soft ground, Joe?'

'Not after a couple of lifetimes, no. But it might put the idea into your head. If you know it's there.'

'Yes. There is such a thing as local knowledge.'

Mabbatt used his skills, gifts, really. He had detected, he was sure, a slight hesitation in Jowett's endorsement of this Jones bloke. He had hardly been supportive of the Major's tirade. An attitude there? 'So you'd say that Mr. Jones is worth paying a visit to? About coin-dealing Josh?'

'You're the detective, Joe.'

15

Arthur Root checked his watch once more as he entered a ginnel strewn with old broken trikes, black bags gaping with bottles and cartons, and one or two junked pieces of smashed furniture. Hagthorpe was not a desirable location. He saw a shadow move, looked up, startled, to see a solemn infant perched on a wall above him. 'You'll fall off, Bert,' he warned.

'Won't. Can't get in. Mum's got key, like.'

Root knew how he felt. He was in a similar situation. Locked out. 'You fall off and I'll be back.' It resulted in the kid flapping his arms and pretending to dive.

The sight broke his dark mood. Mabbatt had been frosty the last time they'd met. But that was the investigative branch for you. Locked out. Maybe he could chance his arm, though, with the gippo kid Josef had rung about. Right.

then, get through to the Rotherham
Trades and Labour Club, where he did
his drinking in the evenings.

* ★ ★

The ACC and Mabbatt flanked Detective
Chief Inspector Turnbull on a small dais
in the incident room and had shown
steady if stolid support as he made his
lengthy presentation, the sixth of the
series: five too many for the Chief, who
became more pressing daily. Things were
at something of an impasse, so Dundas
had remarked when they'd met an hour
earlier.

'I know, sir. Lots of leads, most fizzling
out. And too many side issues, what with
the Wolvers corpse on the one hand, as
you could say, and Constantine the Great
always peeking out of his mausoleum on
the other. Put it together with Danny
Warburton's record, and it's a bit like
juggling jelly. But there is progress.'

Dundas said he looked forward to
hearing more.

The Co-ordinator assured the ranks of

officers that they were indeed making progress. Most of the leads that had been pursued, most diligently in his estimation, had failed to add a great deal to their knowledge of the late Roger Llewellyn Hancock. And the murder victim, Daniel Warburton. As yet, there was a dearth of suspects in the case of the latter crime. And it had not yet been confirmed that the former had died violently by another hand. A process of elimination, therefore, had been conducted. That was progress, vital to any serious forensic undertaking. He ticked off the areas investigated, starting with those that concerned Warburton.

It added up to not much at all, considered Mabbatt.

Warburton's old mates, those that could remember anything at all, had long since abandoned him. He had a van and undertook casual work, and it was believed that he was capable of stealing anything not under lock and key and getting a few quid out of the local scrap merchants thereby: it was in the nature of such enterprises, conducted with a considerable degree of circumspection, so three reports mentioned, that nothing of a criminal kind could be substantiated. And there it was, the Co-ordinator said to a fidgety audience.

'The connection with the deceased Hancock, though, may yield some results. Superintendent Mabbatt will address you shortly.'

It went on. And on, thought Mabbatt. Mrs. Brand had been re-interviewed, as had her son, Gary. Neither had anything to add to their initial statements. The dealer Tolchard in Harrogate was in the clear. All of the business that might be able to add further light on the adaptation of the similar coin mentioned in the paragraph aforesaid had been visited. And it was an appropriate moment for you to listen to Mr. Mabbatt. Questions later.

Mabbatt stood and cleared his throat. He took just three minutes to tell them that a thirty-something bloke, at a pawnbroker's place of business in the poorish quarter of Sheffield called Orgreave, recalled handling an *aureus* when he was just a lad starting out years back He was the manager now, the old one gone with cancer at sixty. It was the old manager who had turned the would-be customer away, wanting nothing to do with the matter. They had done bits of jewellery jobs, not any more but it was another source of income then. It seemed that the old bloke had taken one look at the coin, another at the big beery face of the man who wanted it drilled and threaded with a gold chain, and said, leave it with us for a day or two will you; and then had got on the phone right away and told his assistant that he himself would deal with the customer when he came back: And politely declined the commission the next day, owing to pressure of work. It was this refusal that had stuck in his mind. It was a doddle of a job, and the workbench hadn't been used in a fortnight. 'Someone else obviously did the work for Danny Warburton,' said Mabbatt. 'And it was Warburton, we have an identification by the present manager. But there's more to it. You see, the old manager owned the business, and his widow sold out about ten years ago. Recently it's come to light that he consulted some person. It's entirely possible that he acted on advice given. So who gave it? Who was in a position to say that bargepoles and touching came into the equation? Now, we can see a bit of light, to my way of thinking.'

He waited for them to consider the implication of his news. Dundas had been cautiously hopeful when he'd set it out for him before the daily briefing. 'It could lead somewhere, but consider, Joe. The man's run a reputable enterprise for, what, forty years? More? And it's got to be at the margins of probability.'

There was the added point that Jones would not know Hancock, at least through Wolvers; it was tangential, but a further indication of the thinness of the threads they were picking at. Yet Dundas was still keen on the golf club. 'Things go in circles,' he declared, further mystifying Mabbatt.

He briskly put metaphysics aside and told the ACC exactly what he told his fired-up team. 'We could be looking at a breakthrough,' he said. 'A Mr. Theodore Jones is now the owner of that pop-shop in Orgreave.'

He forebore to add that he was now sure that Hancock's night-hawking had somehow led to his death. It was coming, he thought. You're on the right track. You, Joe, could just make Chief Superintendent out of this.

* * *

Danny Warburton's name came up at not much after the time the incident room cleared. 'I should have put two and two together, silly cow me! Gary, you must think I'm a right idiot — but I got you as Gary Brand, not his son, didn't I?'

They were in the eastern tower's apartment that Josie retreated to when she wanted to be well away from Bliss during her official breaks. It was a strange room, circular, dusty, neglected, yet flooded with romance for her. Where better to bring a lover? Like lovers before they had found an old couch, still gilt and

260

plush red, and now they sat entwined.

At a listening-post he hadn't used in a year, Charlie Bliss seethed.

'He was still my dad, and it's no way to end up whatever's he's done. But he was out of our lives years ago, Josie. And he used to go to your dad's pub? I thought he'd be excluded from the *Hart*.'

It was very much a working-class pub, run by a short, wide man who had bitterly opposed the closing of the mines. He ran an orderly house.

'He used to do a lot of things, Dad said. Kept on the right side of Dooley, that's the landlord. Everybody does, has to, like. Danny hadn't had all his marbles knocked out in the ring. He was cunning. He'd listen and make like he was drunk, but he'd be storing it all up against when it were needed.'

Gary thought of his mother's white face, long ago.

He knew about the Roman coin, despite what she believed.

Fortuitously, he had returned early from the kick-about all those years ago; and heard, through the open back door how his father had tried to make up for an outrage whose nature he didn't properly comprehend until the week before.

'Did he come out with anything about gold coins, Josie? There's some talk he managed to get hold of a load of them more than ten years ago.'

Josie drew him towards her.

'Kiss me. Tea break's nearly over. Well, five minutes then.'

Before they left, she promised to find out what her dad knew.

'Conniving cow,' muttered Bliss. 'Treacherous bitch!'

★ ★ ★

'How do I look?' Ursula demanded.

'Like something from an high-class knocking shop in Soho, love.'

'Good. I was afraid it was a bit tarty. High-class, that's me, very expensive. I need gold shoes to go with it, set off this lovely red, so you pay for your pleasures, Arthur. Me and Beth and the twins are off to look out the charity shops in

Rotherham. Can we have the car?'

Root said he'd drop her near Wool-worth's, then she could get the bus back, which suited the twins perfectly. They would fight their way to the back seat and stick their tongues out at the rest of the Saturday motorists. Beth would sit at the front, fuming.

'Be back sixish,' Root told his wife.

He explained to the duty sergeant that he was looking into a case of shoplifting, and would be back on patrol before midday. What was he looking for? 'Trolleys.'

★   ★   ★

Strapp had tried a dozen times to raise the Jones residence. By ten o'clock, he thought it unlikely that he would get a response. Something was amiss when a busy man like this mega-pawnbroker wasn't either answering or requesting that a caller leave a message. 'Sir, should we take ourselves off to Hooton Pagnell then?' he asked Mabbatt.

'Bloody have to. I want a result on this

one. And I'll get it.'

It turned out badly, though.

The grounds were lush, and the seventeenth-century gentleman's residence more than impressive. It stood in an acre of old woodland, with a small Japanese garden before the mass of the grey stone-built mansion. A black Porsche was skewed across the drive before the wide-open iron-studded oak doors. 'We do see how the other half lives, Mr. Mabbatt. Do we knock?'

Alice Godalming came out screaming.

'How dare you, Mabbatt! Good god, man, have you no sense of decency — I had some sort of respect for you, but now — ! You're as bad as any of those wretches in my court!' She stood gasping and shaking, then she dropped a small overnight case and stamped her small foot down hard. The two-inch oak floor did not shake. Mabbatt reeled back. His big face was florid, his heavy shoulders slumped. To say that he was confounded would be an understatement. Alice was not done. 'Did you come here to taunt me, Mabbatt? Did you!'

Izzy Strapp was rather enjoying the

scene. He had no intention whatsoever of intervening. His boss managed, 'Ah — Alice — I didn't — '

'Know? You knew enough from poor Phil, didn't you! And that befuddled old buffoon Jowett! Asking them what my Ted was doing with that damned pot of gold, weren't you? The Major was appalled when the penny dropped that you were as much as saying Ted murdered Hancock — and all the time my poor love was under so much stress he — aargh!'

Somehow, Strapp managed to get the distraught woman inside.

'Get in. I can give you five minutes before I have to go back to the hospital. But I'll never forgive you, Superintendent Mabbatt, whatever you might say. It's sheer bloody harassment, that's what it is! For all you know — or me — Ted might have had another stroke by now! He's been trying to say something since six this morning, and he's fretting so much I'm trying to do something to ease his mind a bit, and now all you and all this worry!'

'Can we help, Madam?' said Strapp, quiet and comforting.

'He can't talk, he mumbles and he's mad with frustration when I can't work out what he wants, but the nurse gave him a pencil and paper and he managed to write it down, and it didn't make much sense, so all I can think of is that he wants a ratty old dressing-grown he won't get rid of so I'm taking it to comfort him — now!'

But she stayed long enough for an exchange of information.

Silently, and grudgingly Mabbatt approved. She was a tiger, all right. Now, who'd said that recently? Ah, the Major. He appeared in the conversation, shortly after Alice had disposed, scathingly, of his friend Josh Jowett. 'I always knew he was a loony right-winger, but I see now he's a damned fascist! Do you know, I've heard him say that he believes the Germans to be the rightful heirs of Rome — the Hun! No wonder he had it in for Ted, and do you know that Ted was the only survivor of his family? Well, he's going to survive now, no thanks to you.'

It came out in feverish bursts; but it all

came out, nevertheless, for Alice Godalming knew her duty. It boiled down to a simple matter: on the day before he suffered his stroke, Ted Jones had confided in her that he did, in fact, know a good deal about a particular Constantinian coin, since he'd advised a pawnbroker acquaintance, many years ago, to have nothing to do with it. And that was all.

Jones had said nothing of this when the information spread amongst his friends and acquaintances: however, wishing to spare her — me! — any involvement with any form of criminal activity. But when it came out that that young Gary Brand might be a suspect, he had determined to make a statement to you, bloody Mabbatt, as soon as possible. And that was yesterday evening, Superintendent, just after we watched *Eastenders*. 'And when I looked at him in the bed this morning, he wasn't breathing!'

He was, so the paramedics told her. But she would stay no longer. All she wanted to do was tell Mabbatt what she thought of him, and now she'd said all she had to say she was going to her Ted, and if she was caught speeding she'd blame it on him, and don't get in touch with me again. Please.

'I am deeply sorry for your trouble, Mrs. Godalming,' said Mabbatt whole-heartedly. 'If you can bring yourself to do so, please try to tell Mr. Jones that my investigating officers and myself wish him a full and speedy recovery. Thank you, Madam. There will be no speeding ticket, since we'll be leading the way to the hospital. With the flashers on, Sergeant, please.'

★ ★ ★

The walnut-faced little Pole was delighted to see his friend Arthur Root again. Already, a few early drinkers had a pint of Sam Smith's before them: those, who in Josef's opinion knew what good beer was.

'You know, Arthur, I had some trouble arranging matters.'

But he'd done it. This was his trade, fixing. 'So we visit the asylum-seekers' encampment now, my friend? You get to meet this little gypsy chief?'

'After we've had a chat with someone at my golf club, Josef.'

'Nice car. Not so healthy as my Raleigh, but we go in style, yes?'

Josef was not intimidated by the grandeur of Wolvers, not at all.

'Who's your mate?' Freddie Birtwhistle demanded, and when he was told what he had to know, he approved. 'Time they got nicked.'

He was eager enough to provide them with all he remembered about the gippos. Yes, the skinny little brown bugger was certainly the boss — told the others what to do and looked the part, with his gold medallion and his posh blue trainers he kept falling over. 'But 'e weren't skeered of 'Itler, like.'

What followed was gold in itself. Fred had seen the gang flitting along byways and pathways that few used. They led along the meandering river for miles, and they could easily use the old railway bridge to get backwards and forwards to their den. 'Born crafty. Move like so many shadows through the woods. Could be up to any kind of villainy, Mr. Root, especially that young 'un that's got a look of your mate 'ere, foreign like. You going to give 'im a belting?'

Josef directed him to one of a group of semi-derelict Nissen huts on a great, open area of scrub and decaying concrete:

'Arthur, you have what you call a clue. Yes?'

It was a Second World War cluster of billets and the remains of two administration blocks. Odd small sheds lay in weatherworn heaps. Blackened circles of old fires dotted the barren ground. Smoke rose from the iron chimney of the one occupied hut. Root got out carefully and adjusted his helmet. Four small heads peered from the nearer window. A soccer ball rolled slowly from the open doorway.

'The men won't be here, of course. It's just a few women and the younger kids. You stay here, I'll talk. They know what you are here for. Give the women cigarettes, Arthur. That's the tradition — you remembered, Marlboro Lites?'

Two packets, thought Root. That would look well on expenses.

It could be an excellent investment, though. Blue trainers: glittering medallion on a leather thong. All as had been reported, now confirmed.

Whatever they had to tell him, he had been right to tell Bill Brown that he was following up what looked like a useful chunk of new information. And here came the Romanies.

They emerged not at all shyly, an old, very thin, woman first, then one plump and middle-aged, followed by a slip of a girl, heavily pregnant. The four kids followed, led by what must be Rosie's *bete-noir* and Freddie's brown little bugger. Root had been instructed on the etiquette.

'I am Police Constable Root, ladies. Thank you for inviting me to your home.' Correctly, he held out his hand.

The kids held back, three boys, one sparkling-eyed girl the twins' age.

In turn, the women wiped their right hands on their aprons and tried the strength of his grip; their arms were thin, wiry, and without much flesh. They were Mesdames Kalnoky and Pelse; and

Marija, pronounced 'Maria'. In each face, Root saw a hint of desperation and also a good deal of insight.

'Now it's get-to-know time,' Josef, as Root courteously ignited the Lites with a newly purchased green lighter. 'The lady here is that one's mum. He's Vlad. Mr. Freddie doesn't respect him, Arthur.'

'Vlad!' cried Mrs. Pelse, gesturing with her thumb at her son. He wiped his face and winked at Root, then rolled his eyes wildly.

'It's for begging. Vlad makes himself that he is mentally handicapped,' said Josef. Then the old matron said something and turned her back; Marija slid away into the Nissen hut. Neither spoke. Josef seemed not to have noticed. 'These are a very adaptable people. They had to be,' he went on, his gaze momentarily elsewhere. 'The men know you suspect the kids, and they want to make amends. Trouble is the last thing they look for. You will understand, life is not easy for refugees. No papers, Arthur. They want a deal. Yes?'

That meant they'd been pushed out of

the back of a container somewhere just off the M1, like many thousands before them. *So?* Root was engaged, somewhat covertly, in at least one murder inquiry: he would, he told himself, deal with the Devil himself to get a result.

'I'm prepared to listen, Josef. Will you tell Mrs. Pelse that?'

Root heard his name mentioned twice. He thought he may have been instantly promoted in rank; whatever, the exchange between the Pole and the Romany woman proved efficacious. 'It's fine,' his interpreter told Root. 'No one's scared of you. Marija's gone to make tea. You drink it.'

The girl was quick. Maybe the kettle stayed on the fire all day long. The mugs had a remarkable likeness to those used in a large service station nearby 'Thank you, Miss. Josef, will you tell Vlad's mother that I'm curious about the medallion around her son's neck? And that I am not engaged in an investigation as to how he obtained it?'

The terms had been established already. A deal was in the making, had been sealed, really. 'Vlad here, who goes in for the loony look, wants to say something first. Then his mother will speak for him. Please humour him?'

Policing had its lighter moments, thought Root. And just as well, for much of it could bring on the black dog if it got to you. 'Vlad? What have you got to tell me?'

'Iss good,' said Vlad confidently. 'Me Roma. Spik all time Angliss. Him no,' he said disdainfully indicating the others, children and adults included in his wide sweeping gesture. 'Daft buggers, no learn.'

Mrs. Pelse looked to Josef and nodded. He would speak for her.

Trolleys they knew nothing about, apparently.

Mrs. Pelse nodded her head affirmatively. Root knew she was lying, and he knew she was aware of it. Her black eyes held tiny points of sunlight. She could have outstared the Sphinx, which he had seen on his honeymoon by moonlight. Ursula had shivered against him as empty ancient sockets stared at them. The

Romany woman was in no way hostile: she was doing what she could, surviving.

'Josef, please ask Mrs. Pelse to move on to Vlad's gold coin.'

Mrs. Pelse had her hand to the silver chain at her bosom. Emphatically, she pointed to her son. 'Nah!'

Vlad stuck a thumb back in his mouth and did the eye-rolling show again. And again, his mother tried to clout him. Root empathised with her. He pointed to the glittering medallion at the boy's neck. 'Give.'

Arthur Root departed imagining the sound of silent laughter all about him. He had taken the medallion, he told Josef, as evidence, at which the wrinkled brown face creased painfully. 'It's a fine clue, yes, Arthur? Will you drink beer with me now?'

The soccer ball arced into the dull sky and landed near him. Turning quickly, Root chipped the ball back to Vlad and his gang. 'Soccer good!' the grinning Roma yelled. 'Rovram!'

Then he considered the golden medallion in his hand. It had a full-face image of a desperate villain at the obverse. Reverse, a jolly pirate ship.

At least one mystery had been solved.

'I'll drop you off, Josef. Can't spend a chocolate piece of eight at Rotherham Trades and Labour Club now, can I?' And then he stopped. 'Go back and say I want more. Try the old woman, please. Tell her that this is a most serious matter, and that we come back again and again when there's been a killing. Tell her — ,' he said, trying to find a phrase that would ring in the Romany women's hearts, ' — yes. Tell her blood has been spilt. It stains forever. The police in this country never close an investigation on an unsolved homicide.'

16

Dundas had convened for ten. Mabbatt, his Co-ordinator, Tomlinson and Strapp were to attend. It would be a short meeting. And it was. As murder enquiries went, the joint investigation of the deaths of Hancock and Warburton had not been unproductive; nor of a long duration. Once the commonest factor in killings was ruled out — domestic and relationship issues — then motivation focused on the second: basic human greed. At five or six hundred pounds a go, then a potful of *aurei* was arguably worth killing for: to some.

Unfortunately, it had not been found.

'We have a chocolate Captain Morgan, and a stricken pawnbroker who might be able to help if and when he recovers his intellect,' said Dundas. He was neither condemnatory nor over-assertive. Just a bit too erudite. 'Constable Root is to be applauded for his zeal, and Superintendent Mabbatt for his deductions. Will you sum up for us, then?'

Mabbatt drained his teacup and began.

'Well, I can tell you one thing. We haven't got a favourite in the frame Scratched at the post.' The depository had been a blank. Reuben and Royston would bear watching, and so would be watched: they'd got something to hide, and Sergeant Strapp would find what it was in due course. Spion Kop had been looked over. It could have possibilities, and he, Mabbatt was going out to inspect it again later that day. Mr. Jowett was a valuable source of esoteric knowledge and a pillar of the community. Flood control experts thought that Warburton could have drifted along the bed of the Don for as much as eight or nine miles, ten even, which, if so, would mean he'd been chucked in near the centre of Sheffield. The media were restive, but it was not yet necessary to have a circus. No one had come forward yet in response to Lily Ogg's overblown piece in the local rag, which showed Warburton, fists up, in fight mode and then contrasted the pug's impressive physique with a shot of him from about four years ago when he'd been done for assault. Nothing of significance had yet been uncovered about Hancock's proposed emigration to Spanish Morocco. Mabbatt didn't say it, but they all understood that this line of enquiry was stulted. All in all, not much at all, he finished.

'Sergeant Strapp will accompany me to what they call a Pro-am-am-am today, Mr. Dundas. Inspector Tomlinson has a busy time out Barnsley way to check on matters relating to the case of arson in Dore. Can I open the meeting to sharing, sir, as they say in AA?'

The ACC smiled wryly. 'If you think it appropriate, Superintendent.'

He added that both of the victims appeared rather repellent characters.

★ ★ ★

It had been an uneventful morning.

At eight, Arthur Root had already drunk tea with Bill Brown and parked the Megane in the lot at the back of the station. Bill Brown had a few items for him. One or two he should look into that morning. Three break-ins had been reported, and a total of four bikes, two power mowers and a wheelbarrow loaded with tools and gardening gear from the shed it was stolen from, had gone. All would be sold at next Sunday's boot fair, no doubt. The other matter that was somewhat pressing was a neighbours' falling out: two elderly men had rowed over the affections of an old woman a few doors away. 'We don't want any of them in plaster, Arthur.'

Nothing, it seemed, had come of Arthur's report of his encounter with Mrs. Pelse and her son. Root thought it unlikely that anything would. A Cadbury's piece of eight wasn't going to lead to a homicide prosecution. Bill wanted to know how Grace Brand was taking it. He seemed pleased to hear that Ursula was looking after her, in fact she would be at Acacia Avenue that evening to babysit whilst they went to the evening do at Wolvers Hall. Salsa? Well yes. He could, Bill said, look out for a stray dog someone wanted off the street. Honey-coloured and skinny. He had already called the borough catcher, so get a latest location, Arthur.

The day progressed. Saturday was display time for the teens, shopping and chat for their mums. Root saw Beth's little gang in the mall. As he approached, long slender Shahalim O'Grady stubbed a cigarette under a tall sandal. She panicked, decided he'd seen her, waved and gave him a huge smile from perfect brilliant teeth. A flicker of alarm ran through Root too: was it just tobacco? He approached the little group and told Shahalim she was too young to die of cancer just yet. It was a joke, she knew that, but was she aware that he was sniffing the air for the sweet, acrid aroma of cannabis — *skunk?*

Rosie called to him. She was about to light up a cigarette too.

'What about Changie's trolleys, Arthur? He doesn't stop going on about them. They're not insured he says. Tough, I tell him. Well?'

Root explained that he had looked over a likely destination for the missing trolleys, but no, still looking. However, he could assure her that the pilfering would stop. A word of caution had been issued.

'Well, he looked as though he needs fattening, little devil,' said Rosie. 'Kids, eh, Arthur? Changie's not going to miss the odd box or two of chockies, is he, like? Have you locked up someone for doing Danny yet?'

That too was an ongoing and vital investigation, he assured her. She didn't pursue the questioning farther. But she did say something that caused the flicker of alarm he had experienced only a few minutes earlier to re-ignite his synapses. A biggish bloke in leathers had taken to chatting up the young girls. Like Shahalim, for one. He looked back but the little group had moved on. 'Let me know if you see him again, Rosie?'

He went back to his beat. Lunch was a sandwich. Soon the Major would be raising his Purdey to his thick shoulder and blasting away to start fifteen four-somes striking off for glory and a few hundred pounds — the Pro in each Pro-am-am-am team — and, in the case of the three amateurs, a Pringle sweater or maybe a couple of dozen golf balls, perhaps even a swan-necked putter. MacBlaynes' whisky would flow, gratis. And, later, he and Ursula would take to the floor in the huge marquee they'd provided. How, he wondered, would lady-members such as Alice Godalming and her mate Ivy Kenworthy take to a body-hugging red frock barely reaching Ursula's knees and split on the right seam well above them?

He smiled in anticipation and plodded on.

Bikes. A wheelbarrow. And skunk.

★ ★ ★

'It's a bloody carnival, that's what it is,' Superintendent Mabbatt told Strapp. From MacBlaynes' great, sumptuous marquee, set up on the smaller carpark adjacent to the clubhouse, came a pop version of traditional Scottish that that enhanced the whisky-fed joviality of the occasion. He twice refused the proffered offerings, for Strapp. 'Bring him a soda.

Malt, yes. Thanks.'

Some of the competitors thought a sample or two might lift their game and calm their nerves, so they gratefully reached out to tartan trays balanced by tall girls in black fishnets and tartan skirts, confidently standing about on high heels with glowing smiles and low-cut snowy blouses. Mabbatt replaced his glass and told Strapp that they would circulate, this being a party, wasn't it?'

They moved around, greeting this one and that one, all the while assessing and speculating and storing up nuances and squirreling away attitudes, as shown by the more vociferous and argumentative. Mabbatt did not wish to recall the ACC's views on the members. But they would come back. Currents and strong passions, no less. Well, Hancock must have aroused someone's ire. He saw the bar-girl peeping through the window. He followed her gaze to the young lad Root was friendly with. Bliss had had a few things to say about her, none of them complimentary.

Josie saw that the big, fat boss-cop was

watching her, the one Charlie Bliss was scared of. He would be here about the skeleton in the Kop. It reminded her that she had news for Gary. *Gary!* Dad had given her quite a lot he'd want to know. Boozy Danny Warburton was more than cunning she had learned. He was dangerous. She could catch him after he done caddying for Major Wynne-Fitzpatrick. *Yes.* She half-ran to tell her cake-shop friend what Gary looked like, tall, lean, wide and graceful. And about the hard look in his ice-cold green eyes when he spoke about his dad in the secret tower — well, it had almost dissolved her. The grim cop had a hard look about him, too. He was definitely after something or someone. Stone-eyed and very focused.

Bliss followed as she rushed off. *The cow!*

'What!' Mabbatt heard, turning. Passions certainly were surfacing at Wolvers. A well-dressed and full-bodied woman of forty or so, well into the malts, he judged, a bit tottery and spoiling for trouble. She was, apparently, not pleased with what she had just heard. And saw.

'Angela! Scrumptious! Scrumptious and blooming in flaming June like, like — '

The Major had run out of comparatives: ' — like a damned great Christmas fairy!'

Angela Knight had spotted her ex-husband and the day soured.

'A *what?*'

'Dahlia! Blooming great yellow dahlia, that's what, dress and all and you, bright and glowing in — September, yes, right,' corrected Major Wynne-Fitzpatrick. 'Not Christmas yet, right? Get confused. Put it down to Summers here, getting us all gungho!' He gave her no time to accept what for him was an apology. 'Told us not to get complacent, and don't help the buggers find their balls in the rough.'

He was forgotten as she fixed an icy glare on Knight.

'Who invited that toad?' she demanded. 'Phil, I thought we'd all decided he was blackballed. Phil!'

The Secretary was reassuring Josh Jowett that certainly he would not get the yips, just play it one hole at a time. 'Josh, a bit of a twitch before you start is not the yips. That right, Mick — ? I beg your pardon, Angela, did you say something?'

'Say? I practically yelled it, and I will again! I was talking to Alice on Wednesday and she expressly said 'I wouldn't have that wretch in the municipal dog pound, let alone Wolvers Golf Club'. And he's here! I mean, he's not a member of any sodding golf club that I've heard. Can't you run him off, Phil?'

Mabbatt heard that he was entitled to play in today's competition, since yes, he was indeed a member of a club affiliated to the Sheffield Union: not one nearly so desirable as Wolvers, a poor course, the committee perennially short of funds, but nevertheless a Royal and Ancient recognised golf club.

Angela Knight — got it, Mabbatt told himself, ex- of the JCB donator — raised her voice, as she had promised. She reached to a passing tartan tray, drained the glass and took another and went on shrilly, 'I couldn't bear it if the gruesome bastard went away with a prize! Jesus, he's making a fortune out of my dad's yard now the Chinese buy any old scrap that comes on the market! He stole a perfectly good business, Phil! I hate the bastard!'

Mabbatt waited for more, as there must be, whilst wondering what the term 'yips' might mean. The ex-husband smiled back at him, his hands palm up. Knight looked a decent sort. He was well rid of this one. The Secretary was doing a good job on her, though. Better him than you, Joe.

'Maybe we should go inside, Angela — the girl can bring coffee in a jiffy — what do you think?' said Phil Church. 'Angela?'

The malt went down in a gulp. Her hand went out for another, but the experienced waitress had slid away. The job could be fun. Some of the time.

'Think! I think I'm going to scratch the bastard's eyes out — Mick, you owe me! Come with me and belt him one, the lousy stinking thief!'

'Strapp.'

Izzy Strapp deftly placed himself to one side of the outraged woman, whilst Mabbatt pivoted into position on the other. Mick Summers had a look of panic about him, he thought. Was he in line to be Husband No. 4 — it was four, wasn't it, the next slot? Unlikely, as of now. In fact, the pro was still furiously calculating the chances of Angie stopping payment on the large cheque she had just given him to clear his slate. Had she recognised his reluctance to tackle Knight before the two burly cops intervened?

It would be like waiting for the second boot to drop till he knew, he told himself, as they gentled her into the cool interior.

'Ah, tea, is it, my dear?' he stuttered. 'Coffee — Bliss!'

Phil Church ordered every type of refreshment he could think of. Angela breathed hard, then wept. 'Bastard, bastard, thieving bastard!'

'I do have to go, Superintendent,' Church got out. 'You see, it's the scoring. It's a Stableford, and one or two of our team — our representatives — might not quite remember the rules. You see, it was devised by Dr. Stableford to ensure that this form of scoring equalised — '

The Major took him by the arm and led him away.

'Mrs. Knight, can I pour you some

tea?' Mabbatt asked quietly. 'I know it can be distressing after a break-up. Sergeant, do you think you could open a window just here, let the lady have some air and — '

A sharp, heavy report rang out.

'Gun!' said Strapp. 'Shot fired!'

'Go!'

They left the woman and moved with a speed that belied their bulk and years. And they were in time to see a guffawing Major Wynne-Fitzpatrick handing a smoking shotgun to Gary Brand. 'And away we go, troops!' he bawled. 'And may the best men win! — us!'

Two middle-aged police officers tried hard to compose themselves.

'Ah, er, Joe,' Phil Church beamed. 'All well with Angela now? Splendid! Well done! I can tell you it's going to be just like clockwork. Always liked a shotgun start myself — oh, is there a problem?'

Mabbatt decided that he was doing no good at all at Wolvers Hall. It had been explained to him that the sound of gunfire was the signal for fifteen four-somes to begin their rounds of golf simultaneously, each from one of the first fifteen holes on the course. 'You must have had quite a shock, hearing a firearm being discharged if you didn't expect it,' Phil had sympathised. 'It's more economical in time, Joe — we're not as daft as we look!'

That was when a piper stepped forward and began a long, loud wailing, agonising to the non-musical, of which Mabbatt was one. He told his sergeant that it wasn't a carnival after all.

It was a circus.

⋆ ⋆ ⋆

Josie Marsden felt flat. The bar wasn't busy, since MacBlaynes offered free drinks for the first hour after the Pro-am-am-am was over to go with the excellent and lavish buffet. She heard gusts of laughter and hearty applause through the wide-open windows as prizes were presented and speeches intoned by the dignitaries and directors. The Major had a good line in anecdotes, she knew that. His team had lost, but who cared? Gary had had time only to call that his mum was feeling bad, she couldn't bear to go out of the house even though it meant she had to let the Roots down, and she needed him fast. And off he'd gone on his classy racing bike.

'I won't see you then?'

Gary Brand was young and virile. He hesitated. 'I will try, Josie.'

An hour later, those not disposed to listen to the group drifted into the bar, and she had to concentrate on her duties. The noise-level went up. Smoke circulated until it found an air-current and dispersed. She was propositioned a few times, Bliss looking her way each time a bloke leant over to get a look. Then he lost interest. A heavy-set, flashy looking customer, not a member, seemed to have struck a chord with him. They both looked her way, twice, but she barely noticed. Josie had told her mate at the cake-shop that she thought she was in love.

*   *   *

Bill Brown wasn't on duty when the report came in. A younger uniformed sergeant looked it over and said to a woman officer, 'Who was asking about trolleys? Someone.'

It took a few minutes to establish that it was PC Root who had set up the inquiry, by which time his wife was slipping on golden shoes and spraying herself with almost the last few drops of perfume, *Violence*. Then she had to ring Grace to make sure that she was not alone — Gary was back, she called across to her husband, as she reassured her friend that no, the kids were fine, Arthur's dad and mum were delighted to take over the babysitting, and don't worry about it! Just get right! 'Oh, come on Arthur, we'll be late,' she chided, leaving him yet again unsure about the workings of the female mind.

His father took the call as they drove away, and consequently, he did not learn that Mr. Chang was due for some good news until the group at last got round to the salsa he had told them twice already to play next. The marquee was full, the dance floor was uneven, and the crisp blouses of the MacBlaynes girls had suffered. They still smiled, but wearily.

Alice Godalming was not there, of course, but Ivy Kenworthy was. She had been especially charming about Ursula's outfit. 'I just wish, darling,' she'd said, 'that I looked half as sexy as you. Now show us all what you can do. Go on, that's what you came for — go on!'

There was a wait, but Root thought it was worth it. His wife deliberately stretched out a slim long leg in shimmering black stockings. The diamante-studded golden slippers sent shards of light around her. The red skirt split, and he smiled hungrily. 'Our dance, love.'

Quimbara flowed, clacked, peaked, soared and flowed again.

They had been round the floor twice, with only a dozen or so couples up, since the beat foxed most of the members and the guests. Ursula thrilled as she swayed and glided on the polished floor. She smiled at him but also for the scores of males who entrancedly saw her twining around her husband's muscular thigh. Then the radiophone buzzed. 'Arthur, you've brought that damned thing! You're supposed to be off duty, aren't you?'

Away from the uproar of the crowd, he said, 'Good job I had it. And you never are, really.'

★ ★ ★

'What you doing 'ere?' grunted Freddie Birtwhistle. 'If I let dog go, 'e'll bite your balls off!' The gippo kid in the porch of the lodge house grinned back at him. Freddie saw he had a rolled-up news-paper in his hand and seemed to want to present it to him.

'Iss good dog, sir,' he announced. 'Iss 'Itler, no?'

' 'e is bloody 'Itler and what the 'ell do you want, coming at this time — it's near dark, and young 'uns like you should be abed!'

The gippo kid became serious. He thrust the paper at Freddie. 'Iss for poliss. Poliss! For poliss. Big man. Iss Root, yes? You give. Poliss, yes?'

Birtwhistle never conceded a jot, not if he could help it.

'I might.' The kid didn't understand.

'And I might not.'

'Poliss! Root! You do? You do now, sir?'

There was a fearful note in his pleading.

Freddie could respond to a kid who was frightened. Younger than he had thought, now he could see him up close. He nodded, and the gippo was gone into the dusk like a phantom. 'Funny. Tuesday's *Star*? What's so special about that? This time of night? And that sodding row an' all? 'Ow the 'ell does he know Arthur Root's 'ere? Oh, all right, come on, dog. Let's get tractor.'

17

Events moved fast. Later, Arthur Root still found himself somewhat amazed at how speedily the dots began to join, the kaleidocope settle into a recognisable pattern; and the slow and often tedious process of investigation, deduction, somehow came together with blind chance and a good deal of luck, as all began to fall into place.

★　★　★

'Trolleys?' said Root. Ursula shivered in the chill. After a dullish day, the air was heavy with hanging droplets. 'A Singer?'

Because there was a data-link with a Constantinian coin, the chips found that trolleys matched up with various other bites and so in nanoseconds established a connection between a chocolate pirate, a one-armed dead man's night-hawking ventures, a British defeat in South Africa and Freddie Birtwhistle's little brown bugger. There was more, none of it of much value. No conclusions were drawn; but an alert plump young policewoman thought that P.C. Root should know asap and if he wasn't at home, could he have taken his police issue cell-phone?

He was working out how to tell Ursula that they had salsaed their first and last at Macblaynes' increasingly raucous hop. More choices jostled. Get away now and check to see if the trolleys were, in fact, Changie's — Mr. Chang's — property, before going off at half cock and alerting Superintendent Mabbatt to the possibility that there was a break in the current parallel investigations? An alternative was to pick up Josef to speak to Mrs. Pelse for him — again, he could go directly to the barren waste where the kid lived in an old, rusting Nissen hut. He felt a tap on his shoulder, and his way was set for him. 'Arthur, you're wanted.'

Freddie Birtwhistle handed him a fraying *Star*.

'I wouldn't've bothered, but gippo kid were shaking, like. 'Itler licked 'is 'ands.

Never seen that before of old dog. I 'ad a look. 'Im. Seed 'im fight.'

'That's Gary's dad,' said Ursula, wincing. 'Arthur, I don't like this.'

The Tuesday edition of the *South Yorkshire Star* always devoted a good deal of space to sporting events. A soccer shot was at the top of the first page, two footballers frozen in a balletic leap, faces contorted and muscles rigid. Below was the retrospective column: Warburton's two images, superb and at his peak; and bloated and sullen, head still defiantly up though. The gippo kid had found the paper, thought Root, kept it for the soccer image, and by sheer chance picked out Danny Warburton: it had to be the threat, and the promise to keep on returning to interrogate the Pelses. This was an offering, for peace. It must have taken all of Vlad's linguistic skills to add the vital piece. Root read it aloud in astonished triumph: DON METALS. Just that. It was in capitals and shakily penned, but clear enough.

The Roma kid had ringed Warburton's face. DON METALS was immediately below. The implication was obvious. A piece of the mosaic was in place. 'I'll drop you off at home, then I have to go,' Root told his wife after he had given her a brief summary. Freddie listened too.

'I'm coming. It'll save time, won't it, Arthur. Where first?'

Root had already decided. 'The Trades and Labour Club. It's Josef's place of business.'

'You won't be needing me, then?' Freddie said. 'Thought not.'

⋆   ⋆   ⋆

Josie hugged herself. She needed to be on her own for a while, she told herself. The bar was getting to be more and more like the public houses she had worked in, but somehow more disturbing. These middle-aged men got pompous and louder as they soaked up the booze: they seemed proprietorial, as if they thought they owned the place — which they did, in a way — and with it came her. 'I need to pee,' she told Bliss, deliberately crude.

She needed to be near life and music.

Dusk was giving way to night, and the faint moonlight, only a glimmer of white behind high cloud, picked out the pinnacles of the marquee and, in the adjoining shrubbery, the artfully crafted ruins of the folly. Josie sighed, and her hips moved to the rhythm . . .

Rock music baffled the hunter's tread.

★   ★   ★

Josef Grzebieniowski was willing enough to accompany Constable Root and his lovely wife, so young, so svelte, so beautiful. He reached out to kiss her hand, which Ursula thought over-effusive; but then the Poles were like that, true gentlemen. 'I don't want to rush you, Josef,' said Root, who did, and would, 'but this is urgent police business.'

'At your service, Mr. Root!'

He drained the pint glass in one long gulp, excused himself from the circle of mostly men he sat with in three languages and placed a trilby on his short, white hair. Ursula sat in the back of the Megane. Root gave Josef a rundown on what was to happen and had his suspicions confirmed.

'They won't be at the encampment, then?'

'The Roma, to give them their correct appellation, live by expediency, Arthur.' Politely, he turned to include Ursula. 'There must be, as you have deduced, a connection between this boxer and Vlad's friends. It will be a bad thing. But I think this is all you will learn from them. Mrs. Root, Arthur, you see they are very afraid of the authorities. It is their instinct to avoid trouble. Vlad was what you could call a delegate. 'See', he is saying. 'I give you a name and a place. Be fair to us'. And, yes, it is my belief that by now they will have melted into the Romany population somewhere else.'

'We'll see,' said Root, believing him. His destination was a back lane just too insignificant to show on the Tom-Tom. The traffic officer he had been directed to meet flashed the car's headlights twice and Root followed.

'What's this all about, then?' he was asked. 'CID?'

'The Don,' said Root. 'As in Don Metals. Can we start with the Singer, though?'

They had parked the two cars beside an overgrown coppice and had to walk for a minute or so along a track hard to make out even by the light of a heavy-duty torch. 'One Singer sewing-machine, with trolley,' he said. 'Mean something?'

It could. And it did, Root said, when they retraced their steps and drove further alone the back lane to a set of wide gates of metal sheeting that extended for a considerable distance in both directions. A large sign confirmed that they were at their destination: DON METALS. 'Round the back,' Root was told. 'That's what you want.'

He glanced back to the Megane. Both passengers stared at him. He pressed on to a where the newish metal-sheeting gave way to a much older barrier, metal again, but rusting; and with one particular section loose. Beside it half-hidden in a stand of blackthorn, were the trolleys. Each was laden with the marauders' loot — coils of thick cable in two of them, and miscellaneous copper fitments in a third. 'Nicked the trolleys, nicked the scrap,' said the patrolman, so Root was told. 'That do you Arthur?'

The radiophone got them into action. The stove in the Nissen hut was cold.

* * *

Gary Brand was more or less ordered to go and see his new girl. 'Of course I'll be all right, son! She sounds a right nice one. Go on, get off! I don't need fussing over, do I? Just as long as I know you're all right, that's all and not getting into any more bother — you won't, will you?'

* * *

Mabbatt was watching a rerun of the afternoon's international. Wales, for once, had trounced the home country, which did not please him. He reached for the complementary bottle that a MacBlaynes director had thrust in his hands as he complimented him on the security arrangements at the venue. 'Shouldn't really. But I'll take a nip tonight, maybe. And my compliments on an outstanding sporting event, sir.'

And you have a way with you, Joe, everyone knows it.

'Who? Root!' he bawled into the phone immediately afterwards.

'He's found out what! By the Don!'

Strapp, who himself had been drinking the same peaty malt, had been informed by Control that events had moved on, and would he take a call from Constable Arthur Root. So Izzy Strapp had the almost pleasurable duty of telling Mabbatt that a plod had practically solved two murders — or at least, that he had established a very firm connection between Warburton and a large firm of metal recoveries; and one that would certainly have a car-crusher: furthermore, as Root had pointed out, one that might well have had the deceased in its jaws.

'It's pure speculation!' Mabbatt roared. He knew there was more to it than a plod's imaginings. 'Where did he get this cuckoo notion from?'

Strapp ventured that it didn't go

against the known facts, so he listened carefully. And decided it could, just, be. At the very least, this gippo brat had established a causal link.

'Thought so,' he prevaricated. Now what, he pondered, could have scared the whole scrounging lot of them enough to sod off away to god-knows-where in the land?

'You'll be available, sir? If necessary.'

'Hang about, Strapp.' It was coming together, he admitted. Warburton, scrap metal, the Don and a most diabolical method of murdering the poor sod. What to do, what to do. What to do first? Well, make sure the trolleys were hauled back for examination. Look for more, late as it was. Move on to who owned the yard, not easy, not late in the evening. Get onto it, first thing.

'Sir?'

No, not first thing. 'Get round. I can't drive. And before you ask, it's back to the bloody golf club, isn't it! Where else would there be more trouble brewing!'

★ ★ ★

The bike hissed along the asphalt agreeably. On either side, the dips in the fairways were pools of darkness in a pale stretch of shorn grass. Gary felt calm and excited; exhilarated beyond measure, and slightly fearful too. He could see the curve of Josie's neck against the red velvet of the couch in the Painted Room. It worried him that she had not answered on her mobile.

The sycamores fled by.

★ ★ ★

'So, we drink beer at the Trades, friend Arthur, Mrs. Root?'

He was in excellent spirits. Root realised that the drinks would be on him, not Josef, who declared when they left Don Metals that he had not had such an exciting evening since his days with the Stasi. 'Another time, thanks, Josef. Drop you off there, if you like. We're going straight home.'

'Well, not straight home,' Ursula said. 'Arthur, I've done a silly thing. You know that little gold bag that goes with my Scope shoes?'

Root was glad of a chance to channel his racing thoughts away from the Pelses and Don Metals and a corpse drifting along the ooze at the bottom of a polluted river. So, the recycled golden purse, yes? It was absolutely out of the question to leave it in the marquee. No woman would stand for that. 'Josef, we have to call in at Wolvers, then we can drop you off in Rotherham, that all right?'

'Even more excitement! Just like, as you say, the good old days.'

★　★　★

Alice Godalming's call was patched through to Mabbatt a mile or two short of Wolvers Hall. 'Alice — Mrs. Alice Godalming? Ah, good to hear from you!' he declared, sincerely. She sounded neither irate nor peeved. If anything, there was a pleasingly contrite touch to her tone.

'It wasn't a dressing gown — I'm sorry I messed it up!' he heard. Sorry? Then he tensed. 'Superintendent, Ted was trying to tell me about the gold! The gold coin,' she repeated, louder. 'The pot of gold you're all looking for!' And this concerned what, a dressing gown? He asked if Ted was recovering — not ga-ga, he meant — and was told that he certainly was, but the only way he could communicate at present was still only by writing; and drawing, at which he had some skill.

And using it to draw, it seemed, a stick-like Lowry dog with two stick-kids under its belly; but it wasn't a dog, it was a she-wolf, and that made it a part of the hoard that Hancock was supposed to have found. And be killed for. 'Just tell me the nightgown bit again, please, ah, Alice?'

It wasn't 'gown'. It wasn't 'night'.

Strapp heard him roar with delight.

'Got it! We've got the bugger!'

'Still going to Wolvers Hall, sir, are we?'

'Flashers! Siren! Strapp, put your foot down!'

18

The killer was full of malt and reckless malice.

A big, heavy-shouldered man, he could justify any action by a simple reflection on the consequences of inaction. 'Conniving bitch,' he muttered. A rusted length of railing came to his hand without seeming to; it was a thirty-inch section of spearheaded iron placed to keep out the *hoi polloi* two centuries ago. The new lightweight spiked fences were not yet in place. The group in the marquee thrummed out a long riff and gave themselves a pause. He heard the nosy bitch let out a long sigh. She said something but not distinctly. The drummer tapped out a trial intro. It was enough. He moved forward, light on his feet for such a large man. Then the heavy cloud over the moon drifted away, and he could see the terror on her face as she turned her gaze. He leapt, as Josie screamed and instinctively made for people and noise, the hope of deliverance.

★　★　★

'Arthur!' yelled Ursula. He was already moving.

Inside the marquee, two or three fairly sober revellers heard the scream too. Major Wynne-Fitzpatrick was the one who recognised the scream of pure terror for what it was. 'Root!' he called, then louder, 'I'm coming!'

But he was old and overweight and he had to make his way ponderously through a throng of members and guests, and push aside chairs, and then circumnavigate the dais where the group were clattering into a medley of Old Tyme Favourites at the behest of Ivy Kenworthy, who knew what she liked, and it wasn't this modem style. 'Oh dear, Major, what's the matter?' she cried, as the bulk of the old soldier cannoned solidly into her chosen partner, Phil Church.

She was left reeling, with Church putting it together.

Root saw the attacker and reached automatically for his truncheon, then realised that it was to be fists and elbows and feet. The girl was almost up to him, her face frozen in an appeal for life. There was nothing for it but to take the blow on his right arm.

The attacker had speed, and the advantage of darkness from which to adjust his aim. Root took the arc of the rusted iron weapon at the side of his head, slightly above the left ear. He stumbled, tried to hit upwards as he felt himself losing sight of the moonlit folly. He heard yells and the gentle rhythm of an old-fashioned waltz; and that was all. His last thought was that he had let his children and his wife down and that he had failed, appallingly, the girl who was rushing towards him for help. He did not see her stumble.

Nor Gary.

★　★　★

Mabbatt left the car door open. It had come to rest immediately in front of the portico of Wolvers Hall, at his command. Strapp followed. Within minutes, there would be a vanload of uniformed officers arriving, and before them whatever patrol could get to the club quickest.

Mabbatt burst into the quiet bar-lounge.

★ ★ ★

Josie heard the impact of the tall policeman's head on the gravel; she tried to scream again. All she managed was a harsh sobbing cry that could have come from the dark of the wood. The first strike missed her by inches. It was her fall that had spoiled the attacker's aim. Gary Brand's marksman's eyes picked out the whole seemingly frozen assault as he pitched aside his cycle and leapt forward. His boxer's shoulders widened as he stretched out to grapple with the thick-bodied man who had whirled to meet him. Speed, strength and above all the lightning reactions of a young athlete all combined to make him seem like a hawking night creature.

'Gary!' the girl on the ground shrieked, finding her voice at last.

The attacker felt the co-ordination of his own limbs fail him when from the tall slim shape came a vast roaring, echoing shout. It was one word, drawn out and challenging, that defied his threats and shook his resolve. '*No!*'

'Bastards!' yelled Knight as more bodies appeared.

Gary Brand glimpsed an intervening obstacle — Arthur, he saw, not giving him more than a momentary thought — then as he hurdled the stricken man, Josie scrambled to her feet. Knight threw the iron bar and turned. It took Gary in the chest, but he could withstand shock and pain. He drove a knuckled fist into Knight's neck, then tried for a diving loop with his right arm around the sobbing man's legs.

Josie thwarted him.

She somehow put herself between him and his quarry; and he found that he could — just — contain his rage. Then Knight was hurtling through one of many gaps in the broken masonry of the wall, and then crashing violently amongst bushes and a growth of birches. Gone. And the girl was in his arms. Then, when ten, maybe twenty, hard-breathing men and a few women clustered around them all, he knew that his part in the blurred, rushed, two or three seconds of violent action was over. Just like always.

Ursula knelt by her husband.

'Have you got him, Root!' she heard.

She turned a gaze on Superintendent Mabbatt that he quailed from.

★ ★ ★

As with most journalists, Lily Ogg got some of it right and a lot of it wrong; however, she earned the undying gratitude of Mabbatt — and Strapp — for honing in on a couple of phrases that gave a thrilling and even a noble slant to the Wolvers killings. She would never tell anyone who first called Joe Mabbatt a man with the *gravitas* and relentless tenacity of a Roman. But she had to admit — under some pressure from her editor — that it was Major

Wynne-Fitzpatrick who had put her onto the link between Knight's attempted escape and Hancock's death. She was the first journalist on the scene, in time to see the ambulance taking Arthur Root to the intensive care ward where he was to lie for three days before being pronounced out of danger.

Partly because of Root's non-presence, he figured little in her technically brilliant account. She told her readers that greed had brought down three men who lived for financial gain. One of them, a wealthy man, and now on the run was in it because, simply, he could do it. Knight had built his business empire by stealth and theft: he heard of a hoard of Roman gold from the local small-time villain who had not the brains to capitalise on it. Knight found it an irresistible lure. It was a way of using his skills, thereby feeding his monstrous ego. Danny Warburton heard Roger Hancock boasting of his find, and realised that he could easily steal it, because he knew where it was cached: in the very storage depository where he was employed. But four hundred *aurei* were not easily transmuted into cash in hand. He needed an educated accomplice. Who better than a successful and criminally inclined dealer in metals to join forces with? A lucky strike, tell your friends, drop down dead.

Tobias Simmons was out of the way, dead. Hancock had to die.

And eventually, Warburton himself had to be eliminated.

Others suffered and came near death this night, Lily wrote tersely. With luck, this could make three front-page pieces. Tangential bits, plenty of them, goodie! There was Knight's ex, for instance. He'd somehow managed to acquire the ownership of the extremely profitable scrapyard that figured prominently in the case from her father — and then there was a tie-in with the pro at Wolvers Hall, Summers, wasn't it. *Golf pro. A pneumatic ex. Angie, was it? Photographs, then. Summers a gambler, too.* All of it excellent tabloid fodder.

For the moment, she listened, in a journalist's Nirvana.

'It's come full circle.' she recorded on

her Sony. 'Dammit, there's a fine irony in this entire murderous business.' *Irony. Circle.* Lily scribbled the words in a notebook to make sure she had them forever. The Japs' technology for convenience, but batteries could run out: *Pretty girl's ordeal.*

Josie was told she needed a check-up. When she declined, the Major sent for elderly Dr. Joseph Fordham, who tottered out of MacBraynes' marquee, still with a half-beaker of malt in his shaking hand, to declare that all a delightful and brave young lady like her needed was a strapping fellow like the one she was clinging onto. 'Drink some of this, that'll do you. For now. Anyone else hurt?'

Phil Church told him gently that the truly serious casualty was in Rotherham General Royal by now. 'I expect the Superintendent will find someone to drive you home. Oh, there's a bottle of twenty-four year old for each of us, Where's the hosts' barman?'

The Major said they'd all better go into the bar-lounge and have a word with the steward. Mabbatt agreed. There was some serious questioning to do, since it was hardly fortuitous that Knight could have tried to set about the tasty young thing here — Josie — without being pointed in her direction. A sly, lecherous bugger, Mabbatt told himself. Sly and slimy and almost certainly cunning enough to cover himself.

'Oh, Bliss, Mr. Church. Glad the Major called up his name. Time we had a bit of a chat. Clear up one or two matters, right, sir?'

'Just a minute,' said Phil Church. 'Major, don't you think that this young lady and Gary here have had enough for one night? You do?'

He included Mabbatt in the conversation. 'Superintendent,' he said, with the air of a wealthy man who could be jittery but was now the capable and resolute Secretary of a prestigious club. 'As well as Dr. Fordham here, will you make it your business to provide transport for this young couple?'

Neither of them saw reason to dispute Phil Church's command.

'Fine young fellow that,' said the Major

as they left. 'Got a future. He doesn't know it yet, though. He will.'

Lily took down every golden phrase. *A future. Make it your business.*

'Bliss, sir?' suggested Strapp.

Charlie Bliss had a smile that was a smirk and a sly chuckle.

He did not go immediately for the brandy, but he did stoop to reach for an attaché case in brown with gold-inlaid initials, TAK. 'I thought you'd like to know what Mr. Knight left behind, gentlemen. Looks as though he was going somewhere, am I right?'

It was the perfect denouement, Lily Ogg realised. She got the twins at the shewolfs teats in her fast four hundred words for the *Star*, who immediately syndicated the first breaking story as far as Fiji and Finland, the editor gloated. And she got a look at the contents of the briefcase. *Escape kit found.* The Major spoke and she almost fainted with delight.

It was the wonderful climax of his musings. 'Full circle, Phil!'

'Sir?' said Mabbatt, thinking of the headlines Lily would write. 'If there's anything you can help us with, Major?'

'Philosophical ramblings, that's all! The Greeks had the best notions about stories, don't you think? Phil? It starts with Hancock supposedly flying off to the sun with a pot of gold in his baggage. With me?'

Mabbatt scowled. His sergeant looked hard at Bliss, who was grinning inanely. 'With you so far, Alf,' said Josh Jowett. Phil Church nodded slowly.

'So where was our treasure-hunter off to?'

'Ah,' said Mabbatt.

'Marrakech,' said Lily Ogg, who had listened to a good deal of gossip that night. 'Wish I could go.'

'No one asked you,' Mabbatt told her sharply.

'And by coincidence, or maybe not, that's where Knight was booked for,' the Major finished. 'Got a lot to answer for, the goldsmiths in the souk. You seen them trading? No? Hancock and Warburton would have been kids in their hands. Come out in their skins.'

There were seven of the *aurei* in a blue velvet case.

Circle complete? Lily was thinking hard of the follow-ups. *Loose ends? A tangled case* . . . Your correspondent will tell all, as it unfolds.

★　★　★

When he knew that he was still alive, Arthur Root first asked if the twins had gone to school, then if Ursula's red slinky dress was ruined. Gradually, he focused on the two older children, and when he had eaten thin porridge and drunk ginger and lemon tea, he remembered that he was a copper and that drastic events had overtaken him. It was a complex case. More and more interrelationships were revealed. Things slotted into place.

Mabbatt was the star of the show: Lily Ogg had done him proud. He was a leader and a role model for the youth of South Yorkshire, so she averred. His noble profile was that of a rough tribune from the early days of Rome. Maybe a Hadrian. Generally, Ursula told him. Joe Mabbatt concurred. Josh Jowett had been to see him when he was recovering, mainly to tell him that, after all, Roger Hancock could possibly have been right about the Kop. It would bear close examination, because the course of the river could well have changed, couldn't it? Once, Arthur, the promontory may have been a riverside defensive position, yes? If so, of course, that is if he were to make any discoveries at the Kop, then English Heritage would have to be called in, and, well, no more driving-range, you see? It was an intellectual dilemma for him.

Root could live without it, he decided. He was not yet up to analytical debate. Let the Romans keep their Kop, the Coritani their secrets. Life was working out well for the living. Ted Jones — now recovered from his stroke — and Alice dropped in. They thought they'd go and float in the Dead Sea for a week or a year, and perhaps iron out a few of their wrinkles. Perhaps they'd marry too, who knows, Arthur?

Josie wore a smallish diamond on her finger; her fiancé had heard from the War Office and was to be interviewed. The Major had told him that he'd have a rough time at Sandhurst, not that he'd be any the worse for it, vouch for it, worse in my time, evil lot the instructors. Grace had put on a bit of weight and was fretting about it. Owen Burroughs had made a statement and he was doing fine driving an HGV in the valleys. Fred Birtwhistle wanted to see him when he were well, like. Good wishes abounded, and if he got into that kind of trouble again, well she, his wife, wouldn't be responsible for what she'd do to him.

'I'll look forward to it, love,' he told her. 'There's that Singer, too. What happened to it?'

*   *   *

A week later, Knight, in disguise and using a fake passport, was spotted by an alert member of the security staff at the small Doncaster airport. His ears were prominent. The small chubby woman came from Polish stock. 'You got relatives in Krakow, then, Pan Kowalski?'

He had a beard and moustache by then, as well as a thin, worn suit and scuffed old shoes. But he had a gold coin on a golden chain at his throat, which led to a request for his suitcase to be opened. It contained one shirt, a shaving kit, spare socks and underpants and beneath them bundles of high denomination Euro banknotes. Before Knight could slash her with the open razor from the kit, three men had joined Ms. Jarowiczski, who did come from Krakow. 'You are not a nice man,' she told him, when she'd broken his arm. 'You know that? You been in the papers, you know. Pan jest wariacki!'

Later, only a couple of hours later, due to a tip off, Lily Ogg saw it as a part of his paranoia. Knight could do nothing less than exhibit his gains in the traditional way. He was a man who did not believe that he could be caught. Gold, a golden chain, that was his downfall. *Necklet of doom*.

She wondered if the black swan metaphor would swim again and decided against it. No, the *Star* readership could take only so much imagery at a time. Go with *Necklet*.

⋆ ⋆ ⋆

Root was back on patrol three weeks later. He took with some caution his sergeant's news that he would be recommended for a service award. Men and women he knew gave him cautious greetings, as if he had landed from an extra-terrestrial conveyance, not the Megane. Rosie kept him talking for a minute or two and was not surprised to hear that Florrie O'Brien's sewing machine was lost in a bureaucratic fog; then he wanted to go on, to be amongst the plodding familiar. She called him back though.

'I 'eerd about that big bloke on the Harley-Davidson,' she said, not pleased to be telling him this, he felt. Apparently, the biker was trying to sell a very poor grade of cannabis to the local kids, including Beth's mates. But they'd told him to get lost, and he'd not been seen since. Good, thought Root, but good only so far. He turned a corner and talked to Bill Brown for a couple of minutes. Yes, that one had been sorted out. It was the Crakes, who had backed yet another loser. The biker was their runner, though now he'd dropped out of the scene. They'd tried growing marijuana in their battered old containers, but it was poor stuff. 'What they wanted was a couple of terraced houses decent growing lamps hooked into the street lighting circuit and two or three Vietnamese nippers doing their gardening, then they'd have been in business.' And no, the decision had been made not to do them for it. It simply wasn't worth the police and court time. So that was where they were: losers and chancers not even worth prosecuting. Good, or adequate news, then. Root saw the stray dog, saw that she was heavily in pup, and told himself he couldn't just leave her to it. On his way home, he called in to see the greenkeeper at Wolvers.

'I came to say thanks, Freddie,' he told Birtwhistle.

' 'Ope the bugger swings,' he answered. 'Would a few years back. You 'ear anything of the gippo kid, that's what I wanted to ask about — not that I care! Looked thin. 'Just 'ope he lands in a good 'ole, like we used to say. What you got in back, Arthur?'

South Yorkshire chat could be oblique. 'The kid'll be all right, he's a survivor. I have it on good authority, from an expert,' Root said. 'Now in the back it's not so good.' He explained about the famished stray and the two tins of bully beef she's wolfed down an hour ago. It looked like the pound for her, he told Freddie, who could, on occasion, be direct.

Who said, No, 'Itler wouldn't mind a bit of company. Leave her. And a few quid for her grub. Maybe new pup, pups more like from the look of her, tek over keeping young buggers like gippo kid off fairways.

Arthur Root went home to a fine Yorkshire dinner and the news that the dress was all right, but she'd need new recycled shoes before they got back to dancing. The tango was in. 'Oxfam, I think. Five-inch and black velvet.'

Tom, though, ruined his mood.

'I thought about the force,' his son said, breaking off from Sky and Manchester

United. 'I don't know, though, Dad. The way Gary sorted that bloke out — I thought the Army, not just infantry, something a bit special. The Major was Second Paras, wasn't he?'

'Try a parasol,' said Beth. 'Pink.'

THE END